A Candle for Father Joe

A Story of Love, Redemption and Second Chances

Jose Kallukalam

Copyright © 2025 by Rev. Jose Kallukalam
JKbooksthatmatter Publications
Cover Design - Jose Kallukalam
Paperback: ISBN 979-8-9928470-4-8
ebook ISBN 979-8-9928470-3-1

Epigraph

"The light shines in the darkness,
and the darkness has not overcome it."
—*John 1:5*

"Sometimes it only takes one candle
—lit in silence, held with love—
to show someone the way home."

Prologue: The Vigil

The heavy scent of lilies and burning wax filled the air. The side chapel of St. John's Parish was dimly lit, the soft glow of candlelight flickering against the polished wood of the casket. The mourners had gathered in small clusters, whispering in hushed tones, their voices reverent, subdued.

Father Joseph Thomas lay in eternal stillness, his hands folded over his chest, clad in the white vestments of his priesthood. A gentle serenity rested on his face, as though he had departed the world unburdened.

The vigil service had ended, and one by one, people began to leave. The older priests, some of whom had served alongside him for decades, shared brief words of remembrance before stepping out into the night. Parishioners from the many churches where he had served stopped to bow their heads, say silent prayers and make the Sign of the Cross before departing.

The atmosphere was thick with reverence, with a sense of loss.

Then came the woman.

She approached slowly, almost hesitantly, as if she had

been waiting for everyone else to leave before stepping forward. She was young—no older than twenty— yet there was something weary about how she carried herself. Her dark blue coat was soaked at the edges as if she had been standing in the rain before deciding to come inside.

She stopped before the casket. Still. Silent. Watching.

Then, slowly, she walked toward the casket, bent down, and put her arms around as if hugging him. She didn't move for a few moments.

And then, she broke.

A shattered sob escaped her lips as her shoulders heaved, the first crack in the dam of emotions she had been holding back. Then another. And another.

The sound ripped through the silence like something sacred and forbidden.

She gripped the edge of the casket, as tears poured down her face. She was trembling now, her entire body shaking with something far deeper than grief—something unspoken, buried beneath her silence.

A few of the remaining priests exchanged puzzled glances. Others, caught off guard by the outburst, shifted uncomfortably.

No one recognized her.

She was not his family—they knew that much. Father Joseph had come from India decades ago, and whatever family he had was an ocean away.

Then who was she?

An elderly woman, Margaret stepped forward, concern etched into her lined face. She reached out hesitantly, placing a gentle hand on the young woman's shoulder.

"Dear," she whispered softly, "did you know him?"

For a moment, the woman didn't respond. She only clutched the edge of the casket harder as though afraid that letting go would mean losing something—someone—all over again.

Finally, she turned, her face streaked with tears, her breath coming in ragged, uneven gasps. Her lips trembled as if she wanted to speak but couldn't find the words.

Margaret's heart clenched at the sheer anguish in her eyes.

"Are you one of his parishioners?" she asked gently, still holding her.

A long silence. Then, barely a whisper—

"No."

A fresh wave of tears broke through.

Margaret's brow furrowed. If not a parishioner, then... who?

The young woman's hands clenched into fists. She let out a shaky breath, her eyes darting toward the priests still standing nearby.

For a fleeting moment, it seemed as though she was about to say something—reveal something—but instead, she closed her eyes and shook her head.

Regret. Pain. Silence.

Margaret gave her hand a reassuring squeeze. "Come, dear. Let's sit for a moment."

The young woman nodded faintly but didn't move. She cast one last, long, sorrowful look at Father Joseph before allowing Margaret to lead her away.

Behind them, the priests murmured to one another, the same question weighing on all their minds.

Who was she?

Something Father Joseph never told anyone?

Chapter 1
The Fateful Night

The rectory of St. John's parish was steeped in silence, thick with the kind of darkness that pressed against the walls. Only the faint glow of a green LED clock illuminated the room —1:30 AM.

The sudden shrill of the phone pierced the stillness.

Father Joseph Thomas jolted awake, his heart pounding against his ribs. Blinking, he reached for the receiver, his fingers clumsy with sleep.

"Hello, this is Father Joseph." His voice was rough, the taste of night's rest still on his tongue.

A hesitant voice crackled through the line. "Father, this is Gomez. I—I'm the manager at Brighton Motel, downtown. We have a guest here... she's in bad shape. She's asking for a priest. For Last Rites."

Joseph rubbed his temples, already feeling the weight of the night pressing down on him. "Is it serious?"

A pause. Then, "Yes. Pretty serious."

Joseph inhaled deeply, forcing himself fully awake. "What's her name?"

"Catherine Carter," Gomez said quickly. "Father, please come as soon as you can. She's... she's not doing well at all."

Something felt off. Joseph sat up, his mind already racing.

A young woman in a motel room in the middle of the night... seriously ill... not gone to a hospital? It didn't sit right.

"I'll be there."

He hung up, swung his legs over the bed, and hurried to dress.

The Brighton Motel stood on the outskirts of town, its neon vacancy sign flickering against the damp pavement. It was the kind of place people passed without noticing—the kind of place meant to be ignored.

Joseph parked and barely had time to close his door before Gomez rushed out to meet him. The man's hands were shaking, his face pale beneath the yellow streetlight.

"Come, Father. Quickly."

Joseph followed him through a dimly lit corridor, the air thick with the scent of stale cigarette smoke and cheap disinfectant. Gomez stopped at a door near the end of the hall, hesitated, then pushed it open.

A young woman was curled up on the bed.

She was trembling—her thin frame wrapped in a motel blanket, her long dark hair damp with sweat. When she turned her face toward him, her eyes—wide, fearful, desperate—met his.

Joseph's breath hitched. She was pregnant.
And there was blood.

A deep red stain spread across the cheap motel sheets.

A Candle for Father Joe

The moment she saw him, her lips quivered, and she broke down.

"Father... please... help me."

Joseph stepped closer, his pulse quickening. "Catherine, what happened?"

Tears streamed down her face. "Father, I am really sorry. I am bleeding to death. Please give me the Sacrament. I also want to make a Confession," she was pleading.

Joseph's throat went dry. He had seen suffering before. People on their deathbeds. Families grieving over loved ones.

But this—this was different. She wasn't just in pain. She was terrified.

Joseph sat in the worn chair beside the bed.

Her hands clutched at the blanket, her breathing shallow. With great effort, she confessed her sins—a story filled with regret, fear, and choices she wished she could undo. Her words trembled, heavy with guilt.

Joseph's hands were shaking as he raised them in absolution. "Through the Ministry of the Church, I absolve you of all your sins, in the name of the Father, and of the Son, and of the Holy Spirit."

She exhaled—a deep, trembling breath—as if the weight of her burden had been lifted. "Amen," she whispered.

He then gave her the 'Sacrament of Anointing', clearly saying the prayers so that she understood everything.

In a weak voice, she murmured, "Thank you, Father. Now, I'm not afraid to die."

No......

Joseph's chest tightened. She was giving up.

"You're not going to die, Catherine. Stay with me. We'll get you help."

Her eyelids fluttered. She was slipping, fading.

Joseph stood abruptly. He needed to speak to Gomez immediately.

Outside the room, Gomez was pacing near the vending machines, rubbing his hands together. He flinched when Joseph approached.

"What are you going to do, Gomez?" Joseph's voice was sharper than he intended.

Gomez hesitated. "She... she refuses to go to the hospital. Because of what happened."

Joseph narrowed his eyes. "What happened?"

Gomez swallowed hard. "She... she tried to get rid of it. The baby." His voice dropped to a whisper, as if speaking the words aloud would summon divine punishment. "I didn't know, Father. I swear. I only found out when I heard her screaming."

Joseph's stomach twisted. He closed his eyes briefly, his mind battling the weight of duty, compassion, and raw human failure.

When he spoke again, his voice was steady. "You need to call 911. Now."

Gomez hesitated. "Father, I—I'm afraid."

Joseph stepped closer, eyes fierce. "Call them. Or I will."

Gomez nodded, fumbling for his phone. The seconds stretched unbearably. Then—sirens in the distance.

Joseph stayed, watching as the paramedics arrived. They worked quickly, lifting Catherine onto a stretcher and securing an IV. She barely stirred.

As they wheeled her toward the ambulance, one of the paramedics turned to Gomez.

"Police will be here soon. You said she was alone?"

Gomez froze. "Yes. Yes, she came on her own."

The paramedic nodded but gave him a look that said they'd be asking more questions.

As the ambulance doors shut, Gomez exhaled sharply. "That's what I was afraid of, Father."

Joseph frowned. "What?"

Gomez ran a shaky hand through his thinning hair. "The police. They'll think I had something to do with this."

Joseph studied him for a long moment. "Did you?"

"No!" Gomez's voice cracked. "I didn't even know what she had done until she told me! I—I just called you because she asked for a priest."

Joseph let out a breath. "Then tell the police the truth. Let them take it from there."

Gomez nodded but still looked terrified.

Joseph turned to go, his heart heavier than it had ever been.

As he got into his car, he gripped the steering wheel tight enough for his fingers to ache.

Catherine Carter.

Her name would haunt him.

And deep down, he knew this night was only the beginning.

Chapter 2
A Promise Unforgotten

The images from that night at the Brighton Motel refused to fade. They clung to Father Joseph's mind, shadowing his prayers, his morning Mass, and even the quiet moments in his office when he should have been focusing on parish matters.

It wasn't the blood or the beeping of machines in the ambulance that haunted him the most. It was Catherine's face.

That look of desperation. Of pleading. Of resignation.

She had been so sure she was going to die, as if she had welcomed it.

And now?

Joseph rubbed his forehead, sighing as he called his secretary, Mrs. Callahan, an elderly woman with a meticulous nature.

"I need you to record a name in the Anointing Register," he said, keeping his voice steady.

She reached for the ledger, flipping through the pages. "Name?"

A Candle for Father Joe

He hesitated. Catherine Carter. It felt like writing down something unfinished, like a door left ajar.

Mrs. Callahan jotted it down, then peered over her glasses at him. "A young one?"

Joseph nodded, unwilling to offer more. He had already said enough, he thought. The Seal of Confession bound him to silence.

A sense of unease knotted in his stomach as he picked up the receiver and dialed the hospital. The line rang three times before someone at the reception desk picked it up.

"St. Mary's Hospital, how can I help you?"

"I'm Father Joseph, inquiring about a patient," he said carefully. "Catherine Carter."

"One moment, please, Father."

The pause stretched. Joseph could hear the soft hum of hospital noise—distant voices, the occasional beep of a monitor, the murmur of life moving forward.

Then, the receptionist returned. "She's in Postpartum Recovery."

Joseph closed his eyes briefly. She had delivered the baby.

A breath of relief escaped him. Whatever she had done that night, she had survived. And the child—the child had lived.

"Thank you," he said, setting the phone down.

Two Days Later

Joseph hesitated at the hospital entrance, his clergy shirt warm against his skin in the humid morning air. He had told himself he was visiting out of pastoral duty.

But in truth, he needed to see her.

The maternity ward was quiet, the air thick with the scent of antiseptic and something softer—the faintest hint of newborns. He found Room 214 and knocked lightly.

"Come in."

He pushed the door open to find Catherine propped up against her pillows, looking pale, her hair pulled into a loose ponytail. The dark circles beneath her eyes told him she hadn't slept well.

The moment she saw him, something flickered in her expression—relief, wariness, something deeper.

"How do you feel, Catherine?" He kept his voice gentle.

She let out a slow breath. "Fine... maybe better than when you saw me at the motel." A weak smile played on her lips but it didn't reach her eyes.

Joseph nodded. "And the baby?"

Catherine hesitated. "Doing fine, I guess."

That answer didn't sit right. A mother who had just given birth should have light in her voice, some glimpse of wonder or warmth. But there was none.

Then, as if from nowhere, she asked the question that sent a ripple through him.

"Father Joseph, do you remember me?"

Joseph frowned, studying her face. There was something familiar, a distant recollection—but the memory refused to take shape.

She saw his hesitation and gave a weak chuckle, though it held no humor. "At the grotto of St. John's Parish. You told me I had a great future ahead of me. Do you remember now?"

The words struck like a bell.

A flood of memories crashed into him—a beautiful teenage girl standing in the grotto behind St. John's, hands clasped in prayer, eyes filled with silent questions.

Back then, he had watched her from a distance before stepping forward.

"You come here often?" he had asked.

"I don't know how I got here," she had whispered. "I thought maybe prayer would help."

She had been so young, seventeen at most, caught between rebellion and longing, anger and faith. He had sensed her pain even then.

"You're meant for more than this," he had told her. "You have a future ahead of you, Catherine. A good one."

Now, looking at her frail form, her haunted eyes, he felt a pang of sorrow. How different things had turned out.

"Yes," he said finally. "I remember."

Catherine's gaze flickered with something unreadable. "Well, it turns out you were wrong."

A Life Spiraling Downward

Catherine's voice was distant when she spoke again, staring at the IV line in her arm as if the story she was about to tell had happened to someone else.

"My parents divorced when I was sixteen," she began. "They hated each other more than they loved me. I guess I started acting out just to see if they'd notice. It didn't work."

Joseph remained silent, letting her speak at her own pace.

"I ran away from home a few times and got into trouble. Then I found the grotto at St. John's. It was the only place where I could think." She exhaled. "And then you showed up. You told me I could turn my life around."

Joseph swallowed, guilt pressing against his chest.

"I tried," she said. "For a while. I even started praying. Then life got in the way."

A shadow crossed her face.

"I met someone. I thought he cared about me. When I got pregnant, he disappeared. My parents—they wouldn't even look at me." Her voice cracked. "I have nowhere to go, Father."

She turned to him then, eyes filled with something more than sorrow — more than regret.

Desperation.

Her fingers gripped the hospital blanket tight.

"Please help me."

Joseph's breath caught. The room felt too small, too quiet.

He was a priest. His duty was clear—offer comfort, offer guidance and encourage her to seek resources. That was all.

And yet...

Here was a woman with a little child, no home, no family, no support—a woman who had looked at him once, as her last ray of hope.

Though he had once said she had a great future, he couldn't do anything to help her.

If he turned away now, what would become of her?

A war waged inside him. He had dedicated his life to serving others with compassion. But this—this was different.

To help her meant stepping into something he couldn't control.

To walk away meant leaving her to fend for herself.

The weight of the moment pressed down on him. And then, before he could stop himself, the words left his lips.

"I'll help you, Catherine."

She exhaled a shaky breath as if the strength in her body had been holding out just to hear those words.

Joseph sat back, a cold realization washing over him.

He had just made a promise.

And promises—especially those made in moments of desperation—had a way of binding people together in ways they never foresaw.

Chapter 3
A Stranger in a New World

The hum of an overhead fan filled the dimly lit rectory office as Father Joseph Thomas leaned back in his chair, his hands clasped together. A storm rumbled in the distance, the faint scent of rain slipping through the open window.

But it wasn't the storm outside that troubled him.

It was the storm within.

The events of the past few days—Catherine's desperation, her plea, the tiny life now caught in the crossfire of circumstance—had unsettled something deep in him.

And now, in the silence of his office, the memories came flooding back.

A Calling Across the Ocean

It had been nearly three decades since Father Joseph first stepped off the plane onto American soil, his black clergy suit absorbing the unfamiliar chill of a new country.

He still remembered the call that had changed his life—

the voice of Bishop Harrington, a man he had never met before, calling him from the United States.

"We don't have enough priests here," Bishop Harrington had explained, his tone urgent but warm. "Your Bishop, a classmate of mine in Rome, tells me you're a fine young man —full of faith, eager to serve. We could use a priest like you in our diocese."

Joseph's own Bishop back in India, a man he deeply respected, had urged him to go.

"Serve where you are needed, Joseph. You were called to shepherd—not to stay in one place."

He had obeyed without hesitation.

But nothing had prepared him for the loneliness that came with leaving behind the life he knew.

His family.

His longtime friends.

Everything he was familiar and comfortable with.

A Hard Adjustment

Joseph's first years in America were among the hardest of his life.

He had arrived full of idealism, faith burning bright in his heart—but soon found himself battling cultural dissonance, isolation, and a growing awareness of the brokenness around him.

Back home, faith was woven into everyday life—families prayed together, communities leaned on each other, marriages endured through hardship.

But here... here, he saw something different.

In the confessionals, the counseling sessions, the hushed conversations after Mass, he heard the same stories over and over again.

Marriages falling apart.

Children caught in the crossfire.

Families no longer sitting together at the dinner table, let alone at church.

He met teens who used their parents' divorce as newfound freedom—drifting into alcohol, drugs, and unhealthy relationships. Boys looking for identity in gangs. Girls seeking love in the wrong places.

Some children, blessed with stable families and strong support systems, thrived.

But others... others spiraled into destruction, lost in a world where no one was fighting for them.

Joseph felt helpless watching it unfold.

In his homilies, he urged parents to fight for their marriages, to be present for their children, and to build homes where love was not just spoken of but lived.

But for every couple that listened, there were dozens who walked away, unwilling or unable to mend what had already broken.

The Girl at the Grotto

It was during those early years that he first saw her. He could now recall everything that happened, even the very words said.

The churchyard grotto, dedicated to Our Lady of Lourdes, was a place of quiet refuge, a place where the lost and weary often sought comfort in prayer.

One evening, as Joseph was finishing evening prayers inside the chapel, he noticed a figure standing alone in the flickering candlelight of the grotto.

A teenage girl, her hands tucked inside the sleeves of an

oversized sweater, her dark hair falling in loose waves around her face.

She stood perfectly still, staring at the statue of the Virgin Mary with an expression that was neither prayerful nor peaceful.

It was an expression of someone searching—someone hoping for something they weren't sure existed.

He waited a moment, then approached quietly.

"You come here often?" he asked, keeping his voice soft.

She didn't flinch. She didn't even look at him at first.

Then, after a long pause, she said, "I don't know how I got here. I thought maybe... prayer would help."

Joseph studied her. She had the delicate features of a girl still clinging to childhood, but the weary eyes of someone who had lived far beyond her years.

"It does help," he said. "Sometimes in ways we don't expect."

She exhaled, her shoulders sinking.

Then, almost to herself, she muttered, "I don't even know why I'm here."

Joseph knew better than to press. Sometimes, people didn't need answers. They just needed to be heard.

"You have a future ahead of you," he told her. "A good one. You may not see it now, but I promise you—there's something waiting for you beyond all this."

For a moment, something flickered in her eyes—a spark, a possibility.

But then, just as quickly, it was gone.

"You may have to turn a few things around," he reminded her. "Start going to church on Sundays and spend some time in prayer. You will find light ... a light that will guide you in the right direction," he urged her, almost like pleading.

She left that night, not saying anything more.
And she never came back.

Back to the Present

Joseph exhaled, rubbing his temples as the weight of the memory settled on his chest.

All these years later, he finally knew what had happened to that girl.

Catherine Carter.

And she had fallen precisely into the kind of life he had feared for her.

Regret deeply stabbed into his heart. He had seen so many young souls slip through his fingers—people he wished he could have saved but who had drifted away before he could reach them.

But now—now he had another chance.

He had failed the teenager, Catherine.

But he could fight for the mother, Catherine.

And for the child who had just entered the world, innocent and full of unknown possibilities.

He would not let this baby become another statistic. Another child of neglect, bouncing between unstable homes, lost in the world before even learning how to stand.

He had to help her. Somehow.

Joseph knew the risks.

He knew the weight of getting involved in something he couldn't control.

But could he really turn his back on her?

The storm outside grew heavier, rain lashing against the rectory windows.

Joseph closed his eyes and whispered a prayer—not just

for guidance, but for the strength to walk the road he already knew he was about to take.

One thing was certain.

This time, he wouldn't walk away.

Chapter 4
A Line Crossed

The expression on Catherine's face when he had said, "I'll help you," refused to leave him.

It had been fleeting—but a look of pure relief, as though she had finally found an anchor in a storm that had threatened to consume her. It softened the fear in her eyes, loosened the tension in her shoulders.

It had been a look of trust—a trust so absolute that it unsettled him.

Because now, he had no idea how to help her.

The weight of his promise bore down on him as he paced the confines of his rectory. The quiet sanctuary that had been his place of peace and prayer now felt like a prison of uncertainty.

Where could she go?

He had no home of his own, only the rooms in the rectory.

And even if he did have a place, what would he do? Bring her there? The very thought was impossible.

He couldn't rent an apartment on her behalf—not in a

town like this. His collar alone would invite scrutiny. Rumors in this small town moved faster than mercy.

He weighed every possibility—a women's shelter, a discreet conversation with a trusted landlord, an anonymous arrangement through the diocese.

But every path felt like a trap.

Nothing seemed right.

Nothing felt safe.

And beneath all that logistical scrambling, something deeper began creeping up his spine, an unsettling realization he couldn't ignore—he had crossed a line. A line he had never dared cross.

Not a line of his vows, not in the way people might assume, but a line he had drawn for himself long ago: never let someone depend on you too much.

The Church had taught him to comfort the lost, to serve the brokenhearted and to anoint the dying. But there was a difference between ministering to someone and becoming their only lifeline.

He had become that for Catherine. She wasn't just someone he was ministering to. She had no one else. No family. No safety net.

And now—without meaning to—he had become her only safety net.

He wasn't sure he was strong enough to be that.

Why did I even visit her at the hospital after anointing her at the motel?

Did her desperate cry resonate in my conscience?

Was I trying not to ignore the wounded Samaritan on the road?

Instead, I could have easily been that Priest, that Levite, walking away.

Why did I take the Samaritan to the inn, and even

worse, say, "I will repay you whatever extra you will have spent?"

His head spun in the weight of questions.

A Desperate Gamble

For a full day, he juggled his priestly duties while the unrelenting weight of Catherine's need, her desperation, and his helplessness pricked his conscience.

Every moment not spent at the altar or in the confessional was consumed with the same thought: How do I fix this?

He prayed and pleaded for guidance, but there was no divine revelation, no voice whispering the answer he longed for.

Instead, a name surfaced in his mind—Jim Sullivan.

The Chair of the Parish Council, a good, honest man, someone he had grown to trust over the years. If anyone could help, it was Jim.

But what would he tell Jim?

The Seal of Confession bound him in silence. He could not reveal Catherine's past or what she had done, nor could he explain why she had no one to turn to.

Would Jim question him? Would suspicion linger?

Was he crossing another dangerous line?

Despite his doubts, he made the call.

An Answer — a Lifeline

Jim listened carefully, nodding, never once pressing for details.

"Leave it to me, Father Joe. My wife and I will handle it discreetly."

No hesitation. No demand for explanations.

It was more than Joseph had hoped for, more than he deserved.

"Did you say it's only for a few months?" Jim asked.

Joseph exhaled, his voice carrying the uncertainty Catherine had shared with him.

"That's all she would need. She's trying to convince her parents to take her and the baby in, but..." He hesitated. "I don't know if it will work."

Jim nodded. "Let's see. We'll work something out, Father."

For the first time in days, Joseph felt a weight lift from his chest.

A Temporary Home

Things moved quickly after that.

Jim and his wife Mary found a small, low-cost but comfortable apartment and furnished it just enough for Catherine and the baby to settle in.

Joseph went with them once—to assure Catherine she was in safe hands.

When they arrived, Mary approached Catherine with the warmth of a mother, placing a gentle hand on her shoulder.

"You're safe here," she said. "Call us if you need anything."

Joseph watched as Catherine clutched the tiny bundle to her chest. The baby was small, wrapped in soft pink fabric, her tiny fingers curled into her mother's sweater.

Joseph's breath caught in his throat.

This was the first time he had seen her.

A child who had barely survived the choices made for her.

Catherine looked up at him, her voice soft but certain. "I've named her Emily."

Joseph swallowed against the sudden tightness in his chest.

He smiled. "That's a beautiful name."

For a moment, he believed things might turn out okay.

Betrayal in the End

He was wrong.

Catherine's family found out. And they were furious.

They forced her hand and backed her into a corner she couldn't escape. The pressure mounted, and in the end, they gave her an ultimatum.

Sign the adoption papers. Give the child up. Or be cut off forever.

Joseph only heard about it when it was too late.

By the time he arrived at the apartment, Catherine sat motionless, the papers before her, her hands shaking.

She turned her head slowly, her eyes hollow, empty of hope. "They told me I had no choice."

Joseph swallowed hard. "You always have a choice, Catherine."

Her expression darkened. "Do I?"

She waited. Waited for him to do something.

To fight for her. To speak up, to stand up.

But what could he do?

If he intervened, he would risk everything—his priesthood, his ministry and his ability to help others in the future.

And even then... what power did he have over her family's decisions? They would be engaging in an ugly battle with him. And he wouldn't win.

The silence stretched.

And in that silence, something between them shattered.

Her fingers trembled as she lifted the pen and, with a single stroke, signed her child away.

She didn't look at him. Not when she stood. Not when she grabbed her coat.

Not even when she whispered, "I swear, I will never forgive you for this."

Then she was gone.

Joseph stood there, frozen, as the sound of the door slamming shut echoed through the empty apartment.

A hollow ache spread through his chest. What have I done?

He had promised to help her. And in the end... he had let her down.

Not as a priest. Not even as a man. But as the only person she had left.

And now, she is gone.

Probably a soul lost - It ached his heart.

Chapter 5
Years of Silence and Regret

The apartment door had slammed shut, and with it, Catherine was gone.

Joseph had stood there, motionless, as the sound of her footsteps faded down the hallway. He had wanted to call out, to stop her and fix everything—but he had done nothing.

Nothing.

That moment, that unbearable silence, would stretch into years of regret.

A Void Left Behind

The first few weeks were the hardest.

Joseph still found himself glancing toward the back pews of the church during Mass, expecting to see Catherine's weary frame, her silent plea for reassurance. But she never came.

He hesitated every time the rectory phone rang, wondering if it would be her voice on the other end, asking for help one more time.

But the calls never came.

No letters. No word. Nothing.

He asked around, subtly at first, mentioning her name in passing to Jim Sullivan and inquiring at the hospital as if for pastoral care.

No one knew where she had gone.

Her apartment was empty. She had vanished.

And the baby—Emily—was lost to the adoption system, her name buried in legal files Joseph had no access to.

The silence that followed was not just absence. It was punishment.

Haunted by the Past

Joseph threw himself into his work, clutching at the duties of his priesthood as if they could absolve him of the guilt eating away at his soul.

Baptisms. Weddings. Funerals. Confessions. Counseling.

He spoke of God's mercy, of second chances and of redemption for those who had lost their way.

But every homily felt like a lie.

Because deep down, he was not genuine.

He had told Catherine that she had a choice. But in the end, she hadn't.

She had looked at him in that apartment, waiting for him to fight for her, to do something—anything—to keep her from losing her child.

And he had failed her.

The Church often spoke about the sanctity of life and the dignity of motherhood. But where had the Church been when she needed it most? He was the face of the Church for her at that time.

Where had he been? The thought made him sick.

He would lie awake at night, staring at the ceiling, replaying that final conversation, that moment when her eyes darkened with betrayal.

"I will never forgive you for this."

And he believed her because he had never forgiven himself either.

The Journal: No One Would Read

The only place where he allowed himself to speak the truth—the whole truth—was in his journal.

The pages, thin and worn, held the words he could never say aloud.

"I failed her."

"I told her I would help, and I didn't."

"Where is she now? Does she hate me, the Church? Has she found peace?"

"Or has life swallowed her whole?"

And the question that haunted him most:

"Where is Emily?"

Searching for a Ghost

He tried. God knows, he tried to find the child.

In moments between parish work, he made discreet inquiries. He spoke to people who worked in social services and contacted adoption agencies through pro-life initiatives.

But adoption laws were strict. Her file was sealed.

She had become a ghost in the system—a name on some legal document, shuffled between caseworkers, lost in the maze of bureaucracy.

Sometimes, in his darkest hours, he imagined a little girl with Catherine's eyes, growing up in a stranger's home, never knowing the mother who had fought to keep her.

Never knowing that there had once been a priest who wanted to fight for her too—but didn't.

. . .

The Loneliness of Guilt

The years blurred.

People came and went in his life.

His parish grew, and with it, his reputation as a good and faithful priest.

But it was all like a facade, he thought.

He had learned how to smile without feeling, to preach without being convinced and hear confessions without confronting his own sin of omission.

And no one—not a single soul—knew about the weight he carried.

He became good at hiding it. He had to; no choice. Until the day he saw her again after he retired.

Not Catherine.

A young woman, not older than fifteen or sixteen, standing at the reception desk of the Catholic Outreach Center.

And as the past came rushing back, Father Joseph Thomas finally understood.

His years of silence were over.

His regret had found a voice.

And she had a name, as he would learn later — **Emily.**

Chapter 6
To Undo the Past

Fifteen years had passed after all the disturbing events that left Father Joseph with a troubled conscience and haunting memories. He retired from active ministry after being a pastor there for twenty years.

The parishioners had wanted to honor him with a grand farewell celebration, eager to express gratitude for his years dedicated to their community.

But he had politely refused.

Instead, he asked the Parish Council to use the funds for the church's Outreach Ministry—a cause that had weighed heavily on his heart in his later years.

So, with little more than a few packed boxes and a soul burdened by unspoken sorrow, he quietly left the rectory and moved into a modest apartment.

Yet, even in his solitude, the past refused to let him go.

No matter how many years passed, Father Joseph carried it with him—in the way he walked, in the weight of his silence, in the restless nights when sleep refused to come.

For fifteen years, he had lived in quiet penance, haunted by two names that never left his lips but never strayed from his prayers.

Catherine, Emily.

But no amount of confessions absolved him of the one sin he couldn't name aloud—the sin of abandoning them.

Until the day he found her.

A Name Resurfaces

It had started with a name buried in paperwork.

Joseph had long since stopped actively searching—every effort had ended in sealed files, dead ends, and the agonizing knowledge that Emily could be anywhere, living any kind of life.

But one afternoon, while helping at the Catholic Outreach Center for at-risk youth, a caseworker named Linda casually mentioned a girl.

A troubled teenager, drifting through the foster system, unable to find a place where she belonged.

Joseph wasn't listening at first—until Linda mentioned her name.

Emily Carter.

His heart stopped.

"Did you say, Carter?" His voice was too sharp, too urgent.

Linda blinked, caught off guard by the sudden urgency in his voice. "Yes. Why?"

Joseph didn't answer. He couldn't. His throat tightened.

"She's had a rough time, bounced between foster homes. Smart kid, but... lost. She keeps running. We are trying to ground her."

Joseph felt everything shift.

After fifteen years of silence, the name he had whispered in prayer was no longer just a memory.

She was here. And she was alone.

Silent Guardian

Joseph wanted to go to her immediately.

To tell her who he was. To tell her everything.

What could he possibly say?

How could he tell a child that the world she thought she knew was built on a lack of courage?

That the people who were supposed to love her gave her away—and that the one man who should have fought for her stood by and let it happen?

So he didn't. Instead, he watched her from a distance.

From across the room, he saw her for the first time—standing at the Outreach reception desk, her posture guarded, her expression sharp with the defensive strength of a girl who had learned to rely only on herself.

He watched her move between shelves and boxes, sorting supplies and helping where she could. Quiet, efficient, invisible—just the way troubled youth often learned to be.

Linda had been right. Emily was smart.

But what she had said kept haunting him — "bounced between sponsor homes." A sharp edge, but something about her makes you want to believe she can still be saved.

Joseph dared to believe that.

He never told Emily who he was. He never revealed what he knew. But quietly—anonymously—he began to help.

A scholarship that appeared just in time to keep her from dropping out.

A spot in a faith-based foster program when she started skipping school.

She never knew where the help came from. And Joseph never told a soul.

Apart from that, he simply... watched. Prayed. And wondered.

Did she ever think about her mother?

Did she know her mother really wanted her?

Or did she believe what the world had told her—that she was nothing more than an unwanted child lost in the system?

The Unseen Bond

Then — one evening, it happened.

Emily Carter met Father Joseph for the first time.

It was purely by accident.

Emily had been volunteering at the Diocesan Outreach Center, mainly for the service hours she needed to graduate high school.

She wasn't religious. Didn't believe in God.

But the space felt safe. Calmer than most places she had known.

And there was something about the older priest who worked quietly in the background. He seemed to notice things no one else did.

She couldn't explain it, but every time he spoke, she felt something stir inside her — something she didn't understand.

A strange... familiarity. Like she knew him.

Like he had always known her.

. . .

In the evening, after a long shift at the Diocesan Outreach center, Emily lingered behind while the other volunteers left.

She approached Joseph as if wanting to ask something.

When Joseph saw her right before him, he felt he was losing himself.

It had been one thing to help her from the shadows. But now, she was right in front of him, asking questions.

"Father Joseph?" she asked hesitantly.

He turned his attention to her from the stack of books he had been shelving.

She hesitated, then shook her head. "Never mind."

Joseph put down the book in his hands. "What is it, Emily?"

She fidgeted, arms crossed. "You ever look at someone and feel like... you've known them forever?"

His chest tightened. He forced a small smile. "Sometimes."

Emily nodded slowly, her gaze searching his face. "You ever wonder why some people cross your path?" she asked.

Joseph exhaled. "I think... every person we meet has a purpose in our lives. Even if we don't understand it at first."

Emily gave a small, sad smile. "Yeah... maybe."

Then she walked away.

Joseph watched her go, his heart pounding.

He knew.

He knew the time was coming when he would have to tell her the truth.

He had spent fifteen years running from it.

But the past had found him again.

And this time... He couldn't walk away.

God has offered me another chance, he thought.

Chapter 7
A Wounded Heart

Father Joseph arrived at the Diocesan Outreach Center earlier than usual, though he wasn't sure why.

Maybe it was routine. Perhaps it was with some hope.

As he worked alongside the other volunteers—sorting food items, hanging clothes on racks, arranging supplies for those in need—his eyes kept scanning the room, searching.

Searching for her.

But the morning passed without a single glimpse of Emily Carter.

By early afternoon, he tried to focus on his tasks, pushing down the disappointment creeping into his chest.

Maybe she wouldn't come today.

Maybe she was just another unsteady youth, never prompt.

And then—just as he had given up hope—she appeared.

She walked in casually, a small purse slung over her shoulder, her movements light but detached, as if the world carried no weight on her shoulders—or as if she had long since grown used to carrying it.

Joseph's heart leaped momentarily before forcing himself to remain composed.

She walked over to the manager, received her assignment, and immediately got to work, moving through the aisles with effortless precision.

Joseph observed her from a distance. She was smart. Sharp. Capable.

And yet, there was something about her—a restlessness, a distance in her eyes, a lack of attachment to anything around her.

If only someone could love her. If only someone could guide her in the right direction.

A deep sigh escaped him. But he wasn't sure if he had that right anymore.

An Invitation

By the time evening rolled around, most of the volunteers had trickled out one by one, their shifts completed.

Joseph lingered, still stacking shelves when he noticed Emily walking past him.

She caught his gaze, and—for the first time—she smiled —a small, fleeting smile.

"How are you, Father?" Her voice was light, but something about it felt... careful.

Joseph returned the smile. "I'm fine, Emily."

He hesitated, then asked, "Do you care for a cup of coffee after we finish?"

She turned her head slightly, as if weighing the request, then gave a slight nod.

"Sure. I'll meet you in the dining area."

With that, she turned away, heading toward the supply closet with an armful of donations.

Joseph watched her go, feeling a strange mix of relief and unease.

Something about tonight felt... different.

A Quiet Moment

The outreach center was quiet now, emptied for the night, save for the two of them.

Father Joseph and Emily Carter sat across from each other, their coffee cups resting between them, the steam curling into the dimly lit air.

She had agreed to meet him—though even she wasn't entirely sure why.

It could be curiosity. Maybe it was the fact that he seemed different from the others—less judgmental, less eager to fix her.

Maybe, just maybe, she was desperate for someone to listen.

Joseph took a sip of his coffee before breaking the silence. "How are your studies going?"

Emily exhaled, rolling her eyes slightly. "Usual."

She tapped a finger against the coffee cup absentmindedly.

"Sometimes, I get these bursts of motivation, and I do well. I actually care. Then, other times, I just think, 'What's the point? My life isn't going anywhere anyway.' And everything goes down the drain."

She made a dramatic thumbs-down gesture.

Joseph chuckled softly. "So that means you're intelligent. You just need a little encouragement."

"Who cares, Father?" She shrugged, forcing a hollow smile as she looked away.

Joseph's expression softened. "What if someone does?"

She turned back to him, startled.

For a moment, she simply stared at him, unsure how to respond.

She had spent her entire life assuming no one did. No one ever had.

The thought that someone might actually care—that this priest, of all people, might care—unnerved her.

"Why would you?" she asked, her voice quieter now.

Joseph leaned forward slightly, his gaze steady. "Because no one should feel like they don't matter, Emily."

She swallowed, shifting in her seat.

This was it.

The moment she had been waiting for — the chance to say everything she had never dared to say. Now, someone was willing to listen to her.

She had agreed to meet with him, hoping she would get a chance to vent out her pent-up frustrations.

And yet, now that the moment had come, she hesitated —as if dragging the words out of herself would be just another reminder of the life she had never asked for.

Her fingers traced the handle of the coffee mug, and then, without looking up, she whispered:

"I have tried everything bad in life, Father."

Joseph swallowed his throat tight. He didn't rush her. He let the words fall as they came, raw and unfiltered.

Emily exhaled sharply, shaking her head as if disgusted with herself.

"I am sorry, but that's what life has offered me."

She gave a hollow laugh, but there was no humor in it. Only bitterness. Only pain.

"I don't know where to start. Maybe I was doomed from the beginning. Maybe some people just aren't meant for... for good things."

She finally looked at him then, her eyes tired, guarded, yet desperate for someone to understand.

"I never had anyone who genuinely cared. Not once. Not ever."

Joseph felt the words like a blow to his chest.

She dropped her gaze again. "Foster homes... they were all the same. I went from one place to another, people taking me in because they got a check at the end of the month. No one ever wanted me. Not really."

Her voice trembled, but she fought against it. "I learned quickly—if I was quiet, they left me alone. They passed me off to the next family if I got into trouble. If I cried, no one listened."

A bitter smile crossed her face. She looked straight into Joseph's eyes, "You ever cry yourself to sleep, Father? And wake up in a bed that isn't yours, in a house full of strangers, and realize—this is your life? That there's no one coming to take you home?"

Joseph opened his mouth, but no words came.

Emily laughed again, shaking her head. "I stopped waiting for someone to come for me. I stopped believing there was anyone out there who gave a damn. And when you stop believing... you stop caring. About yourself. About life."

She sat back, arms crossed. "I got through the system by doing whatever it took to survive. If that meant lying, stealing, drinking—so be it. If that meant taking a hit so someone else wouldn't, fine. I just stopped feeling."

She looked past him as if staring into the past, reliving moments he could never see.

"I tried everything. Everything that numbed me. Alcohol, drugs, bad relationships. I ran away more times than I can count. It didn't matter where I went—everywhere felt the same. Meaningless. Cold."

Joseph clenched his fists beneath the table, fighting back the helpless rage that swelled within him.

"I got into trouble with the law. Petty stuff at first—shoplifting, skipping school, sneaking into bars when I was too young. Then, bigger things. I spent time in juvie. They said I was out of control."

She let out a short breath, shaking her head. "You want to know the funny thing? I wasn't angry. I wasn't even rebellious. I just... didn't care. When you have nothing to lose, nothing really matters."

Her voice cracked then, ever so slightly.

"I watched other kids—kids with families, kids with someone to call when things got bad. I watched them go home at the end of the day. And I realized—I didn't have a home. I didn't have anyone."

A long silence settled between them. Then she whispered, "I don't even know why I'm telling you this."

Joseph exhaled, steadying himself. "Because deep down, Emily, you want to believe someone cares."

She met his gaze, something flickering in her expression —doubt, hope, exhaustion, all tangled together.

"Do they?" she asked softly. "Do you?"

Joseph felt a lump in his throat. "Yes." His voice was firm, steady. "I do."

Emily looked at him for a long moment, searching for the lie she had always expected from others.

But this time, looking at his compassionate face, she thought he was genuine.

She blinked quickly as if trying to shake off whatever emotion threatened to surface.

Then she sat back, crossing her arms again, retreating into herself. "Well. It doesn't change anything."

But Joseph saw it—the slightest crack in the walls she had spent years building. And in that crack, a glimmer of something he hadn't seen before.

"What if we can change things around?" Joseph's voice was firm.

Her eyes told him she still wanted to be saved. There was a flicker of something in her eyes.

Chapter 8
A Path to Redemption

Father Joseph returned to his small, quiet apartment that night with a feeling he hadn't experienced in years—purpose.

For so long, he had carried the weight of regret, trapped in a cycle of remembering what he had lost. But now, for the first time, he felt he could finally do something right.

Emily had looked at him with doubt, suspicion, and even defiance—but beneath all that, there had been something else.

A flicker of hope. And he couldn't back away this time.

A Plan Forms

The whole night, he lay awake, running through possibilities in his mind.

How could he pull Emily out of this vicious cycle?

He had already researched grants and financial aid for adopted children who had aged out of the system. The State had programs to help young adults build a stable future—if only someone guided them toward it.

Joseph turned on his desk lamp and shuffled through a stack of papers he had gathered over the years—resources he had once hoped to use for other struggling youth but had never found the right opportunity.

Now, he had someone to fight for.

And then, a name surfaced in his mind.

Jim.

Jim Sullivan.

Joseph sat up straighter. Of course. Jim had always been a man who got things done.

A devoted alumni of State University, Jim sat on the Advisory Board, gave periodic lectures, and even established an endowment fund for underprivileged students.

Bingo. There it is.

If Emily could finish high school with strong grades, she had a real chance at a scholarship. A chance at a future she had never dared to dream of.

For the first time in a long, long time, Joseph felt at peace.

That night, he slept like a child.

The Proposal

The very next day, Joseph met with Jim and Mary Sullivan.

When Jim opened the door to his home, his eyes widened in recognition. "Father Joe! Well, this is a surprise."

Joseph stepped inside, suddenly realizing how long it had been since he had last visited.

Mary soon joined them, offering him tea. "It's been years, Father. How have you been? Is retirement doing you good?"

"Oh, yeah. I am enjoying my retirement. But I am also busy in some ways. I volunteer at some of the outreach centers." Joseph smiled.

Then, he took a deep breath before speaking. "Do you remember Catherine? And the child?"

The room fell silent for a moment.

Jim nodded slowly. "Of course we do. Wasn't it a long time ago? I remember. We helped you find that apartment for them. But then... she disappeared, right?"

Joseph's throat tightened. "Yes, you're right. That child, Emily... I found her."

Mary's hand went to her chest. "Oh, dear."

Jim leaned forward, curiosity and concern etched across his face. "And?"

Joseph explained everything.

How Emily had been lost in the system, moving between foster homes, how she had drifted into a reckless lifestyle, and how she had nearly given up hope.

"She's bright," he added, "but she doesn't believe in herself. She thinks her future is already written."

Jim rubbed his chin thoughtfully. "But you think she can turn things around?"

"I know she can," Joseph said firmly. "She just needs someone to believe in her. Someone to give her a chance."

Jim exchanged a glance with Mary, then nodded thoughtfully.

"It's definitely doable, Father. If she finishes strong this year and scores reasonably well on her SATs, we can get her a full scholarship at State University—tuition, books, housing, the whole package."

Joseph felt his chest tighten with emotion.

"I don't know how I can thank you enough," he murmured, blinking rapidly.

Jim waved him off. "You don't need to thank me. Just make sure she believes in herself."

. . .

The Challenge

Later that evening, Joseph sat across from Emily once again in a quiet corner of the outreach center's dining hall.

There was no small talk this time. He looked her straight in the eyes.

"Emily, I'm going to challenge you to something."

She raised an eyebrow, intrigued but skeptical. "A challenge?"

Joseph nodded. "I want you to think about your life—not the past, not the pain—but what your future could be."

Emily scoffed. "Future? Yeah, right. What kind of future do you think I have, Father?"

"You have two choices," he said calmly.

"Either continue living like you are now, floating aimlessly and ending up where life tosses you... or show the courage to take control and build the life you've always wanted—a university education, a good career, a family who loves you."

Emily laughed bitterly. "Oh, what an impossible dream, Father."

"What if I told you it wasn't impossible?" he countered. "What if I told you that if you work hard this year, we could secure you a full college scholarship?"

Her laughter stopped.

She stared at him, searching his face, waiting for the catch.

"College?" she repeated, almost like the word was forbidden. "No way, Father. How would I pay for that?"

Joseph smiled. "You won't have to. I spoke with someone at State University. They have endowment funds for students like you. If you finish high school strong, we can get you in."

Emily sat in silence. That was something she had never considered.

Her whole life, she had been surviving—never planning, never dreaming.

And now, this priest was suddenly telling her that there was something more?

That she was worth more?

Her mind raced. Does someone actually care about me? My future?

Is this priest crazy? Or maybe... honest, for a change?

She stood abruptly, walking toward the door, her thoughts spinning.

Joseph didn't stop her.

Just as she reached the doorway, she turned back.

She met his gaze, and for the first time, there was something in her eyes that wasn't sarcasm, or pain, or anger.

Hope. A small, fragile hope.

"What if I accept the challenge, Father Joe?" she asked quietly.

Joseph's heart swelled. She called him Father Joe, a name only his best friends used.

He wanted to stand up, wanted to tell her this was the moment she was choosing a different path, wanted to embrace her like a father would a lost child.

Instead, he simply smiled.

She gave him one last glance before stepping out the door.

Joseph exhaled, closing his eyes for a brief moment.

This was the first step.

And maybe—just maybe—it wasn't too late to undo the past.

Chapter 9
A Transformation Begins

Father Joseph had always believed in the power of redemption. He had preached about it, counseled broken souls about it, and prayed for it in the solitude of his small apartment.

But now, for the first time in years, he was witnessing it unfold before his very eyes.

Emily Carter had accepted his challenge. And she was going to turn her life around.

She still volunteered at the Catholic Outreach Center, but it wasn't for service hours this time.

She was there because she wanted to be.

She worked with a newfound sense of purpose, sorting through donations with care and assisting struggling families with genuine compassion.

And, perhaps more than anything, she wanted to see Father Joseph.

Emily always had something new to tell him—a class she excelled in, a subject she found interesting, a book she had picked up from the library.

Some days, she would insist on taking him out to lunch,

dragging him to a tiny café near the center where she'd chatter excitedly about her studies between bites of pasta or soup.

"You know, Father, I always thought school was a joke. Turns out, I'm actually smart," she'd say with a mischievous grin.

Joseph would chuckle. "I always knew that, Emily."

She would roll her eyes. "Well, you had way too much faith in me."

And yet, for the first time in her entire life, she was beginning to have faith in herself, too.

A Bond Strengthened

Joseph watched over her carefully, not in a controlling way, but as a quiet presence in her life—someone she could count on.

Emily would call him on the days he wasn't at the Outreach Center.

"Hey, Father Joe, guess what? I got an A on my math test. And I didn't even cheat this time!"

He had laughed at that. "Emily, you shouldn't have been cheating in the first place."

"I know, I know," she'd say dramatically. "That was the old me. The new me is practically a saint."

He couldn't help but smile at her playful sarcasm. "Do you want me to recommend your name for canonization?"

"Really? Do you have connections?" She added to his playfulness.

And then, some days, her calls were different. "Father Joe… do you ever wonder why some people get good parents and some don't?"

Joseph's grip on the phone would tighten. "Yes, Emily. I do."

There were moments he thought about telling her the

truth—about Catherine, about the night she had been forced to sign the adoption papers.

But it never felt like the right time. He had promised himself that he would tell her only when it wouldn't break her.

And for now, she was finally healing. He wouldn't jeopardize that.

The Reward of Redemption

In the end, her hard work paid off.

To the shock of her teachers, foster care supervisors, and even herself, Emily graduated with exceptional grades.

Joseph wasted no time. He took her straight to Jim and Mary Sullivan, who had always been ready to help. They were seeing her for the first time after that fateful day.

Jim listened carefully, his expression unreadable, before finally nodding. "Well, Father Joe, I'd say you've got a remarkable young woman here."

Emily, sitting beside Joseph, shifted uncomfortably. "I mean... I guess."

Jim chuckled. "You don't have to be modest. You've come a long way, kid."

With Jim's guidance and connections, everything fell into place faster than Emily could have imagined.

The Diocesan Social Outreach Center quietly took care of the necessary formalities—guardianship, paperwork, even her release from the state system.

No headlines. No courtroom drama. Just a few signatures, some discreet conversations... and a girl finally claimed by someone who truly cared.

And for the first time in her life, Emily belonged somewhere—not just on paper, but in someone's heart.

. . .

She got admitted into the State University —not just with a partial scholarship, but a full one. Everything—tuition, housing, meals, books—was covered, as Jim had promised.

When she received the confirmation letter, she stared at it in disbelief. "This... this can't be real," she whispered, clutching the paper like it might disappear.

Joseph placed a gentle hand on her shoulder. "It's real, Emily. You've earned this."

She swallowed hard, blinking against the tears welling in her eyes. No one had ever said those words to her before.

And to her disbelief, she truly believed them.

A Goodbye Marked by Love

The Sunday evening before she left for University, Emily stopped by Joseph's apartment.

She didn't say much at first—just stood at the door, fidgeting with the strap of her bag.

Then, without warning, she stepped forward and hugged him.

Tight.

Fiercely.

Stunned, Joseph froze for a second, before slowly wrapping his arms around her. He could feel her shoulders shaking.

When she pulled back, tears streamed down her cheeks.

"Father Joe," she whispered, her voice raw with emotion, "I did something without asking your permission."

He frowned slightly. "What is it?"

Emily hesitated, biting her lip before finally saying,

"When I filled out my University application... I put your name as my parent."

Joseph felt his heart stop. His vision blurred, his throat tightened, and he suddenly found it difficult to breathe.

For a moment, he couldn't speak. And then, in the softest, most fragile voice, he whispered: "Emily..."

She forced a weak smile through her tears. "I hope that's okay."

Joseph swallowed the overwhelming emotions threatening to break him and nodded, blinking rapidly.

"It's more than okay, dear." He smiled, "Now I have a daughter."

She exhaled, relief washing over her face.

Joseph cleared his throat, forcing himself to steady his voice. "Emily, God cares about you. That's what this means."

He looked at her before continuing. "And I think it's a good idea for you to get involved in a church community at the University. Faith-based student groups can be a great support system. You'll meet good people."

She let out a soft laugh. "I don't know about all that, Father."

"You'll see," he said gently. "You won't feel alone anymore."

For a fleeting moment, Joseph hesitated.

Should he tell her?

Should he finally reveal who she was... where she came from... what he had failed to do for her mother?

But looking at her now—so full of hope, full of life, full of potential—he knew.

Now was not the time. She was ready for a future.

And the past... could wait.

Emily left with a heart full of hope for the first time in her life.

And Joseph stood at the door long after she was gone, his soul heavy with both love and regret.

He had given her a future. But the past still loomed behind them both.

And one day, he would have to face it.

Chapter 10
A Night to Remember

The evening before Emily left for University, Father Joseph wanted to give her something she had never had before.

A night where she didn't have to wonder where she belonged.

A night where she felt loved, celebrated, and seen.

A night where she could sit among people who truly cared about her—as if she were family.

And so, he arranged a special dinner at one of the finest restaurants in town, a place Emily had never even imagined stepping into.

And to make the evening even more meaningful, he invited Jim and Mary Sullivan. They had been part of her story long before she ever knew it.

But tonight, they wouldn't speak of the past.

Tonight, it was about her future.

A Night of Firsts

When Emily stepped into the restaurant, she paused at the entrance.

The warm glow of chandeliers, the soft hum of conversation, and the scent of fine cuisine filling the air—it was unlike anything she had ever experienced.

She hesitated, adjusting the simple but elegant dress she had picked for the occasion.

She turned to Joseph, eyes wide. "Are you sure we're allowed to be here, Father?"

Joseph chuckled. "Of course, Emily. This night is for you."

She bit her lip, still overwhelmed. "It just feels... too fancy. I don't belong in places like this."

Joseph stopped and placed a reassuring hand on her shoulder. "You belong anywhere you choose to be. Never let anyone make you feel otherwise."

She swallowed hard, nodding, and allowed him to lead her inside.

As they reached their table, Jim and Mary stood to greet them.

Jim, ever the gentleman, extended a hand with a warm smile. "So, here we meet again the remarkable young woman we've been hearing a lot about."

Emily shook his hand, feeling both shy and deeply grateful.

Mary pulled her into a gentle embrace. "We are so proud of you, dear."

Emily blinked rapidly. She wasn't used to this—people being proud of her.

As they all settled in, the evening unfolded with a warmth Emily hadn't known in all her seventeen years of life.

. . .

A Family She Never Had

Jim and Mary listened intently as Emily talked about her high school journey, her new excitement for learning, and the hopes she never thought she'd have.

At one point, Jim chuckled, shaking his head. "I have to admit, I was skeptical at first when Father Joe came to me with this idea. But now, seeing you here, I have no doubt—he saw something in you that you didn't even see in yourself."

Emily smiled sheepishly. "I think Father Joseph is way too optimistic sometimes."

Mary laughed. "Or maybe he just has a Shepherd's heart, knowing his sheep."

Joseph shifted uncomfortably, trying to deflect the attention, but Jim raised a glass in his direction.

"To Father Joe—the heart of a true Shepherd of Christ."

The words hit Joseph deeply.

He wasn't a perfect shepherd. He had failed once before, and that failure still weighed on him every single day.

But looking at Emily now—confident, hopeful, full of life—he realized that maybe, just maybe, God had given him a second chance to be one.

Emily clinked her glass of sparkling water with theirs, her voice softer now.

"To all of you... for everything you've done for me."

Joseph swallowed, willing himself to keep his emotions in check.

Farewell, Not Goodbye

As the evening came to an end, Jim reached for the check, waving off Joseph's protest.

"Absolutely not, Father," Jim said firmly. "This is my way of thanking you. You've given Emily a future. That's priceless."

Emily turned to Jim and Mary, her voice suddenly thick with emotion. "I don't know how to thank you both. For this night. For everything."

Mary touched her hand gently. "Just promise us one thing—keep believing in yourself."

Emily nodded quickly. "I will."

As they stepped outside into the cool night air, Joseph could sense the heaviness in Emily's silence.

She had never had a night like this before. She had never felt like she truly belonged.

And as they stood outside the restaurant, looking at the stars, she finally whispered, "This was the best night of my life."

Joseph smiled, swallowing the lump in his throat.

"It's only the beginning, Emily. The best is yet to come."

She turned to him, her eyes glistening.

She truly believed it.

Chapter 11
Emily's New World

Emily Carter stepped onto the University campus, her duffel bag slung over her shoulder, her heart pounding with nervous excitement.

Everything was new. The massive buildings, the buzzing sidewalks, the thousands of students—each seemingly knowing exactly where they belonged.

For a moment, she felt like an imposter. Then, she heard Father Joseph's voice in her mind.

"Emily, God cares about you. That's what this means."

She took a deep breath and squared her shoulders. "Alright, University. Let's do this."

The dorm was nothing like the places she had lived before—not the foster homes, not the temporary apartments, not the Outreach Center.

It was hers. Her own little space, her own desk, her own bed, even a shared mini-fridge with her roommate—a lively girl named Jessica, who had an infectious laugh and a closet filled with clothes Emily could never dream of affording.

"You're my new project, Emily," Jessica had declared

after ten minutes of knowing her. "We are getting you a social life."

Emily had laughed, shaking her head. "I'm here for the academics, Jess. Not for the drama."

"Academics AND fun," Jessica corrected. "Trust me, you'll thank me later."

Emily the Role Model

True to her promise, Emily threw herself into her studies. Her classes were intense, the professors demanding, and the readings endless—but she loved every second of it.

For the first time in her life, she felt like she was exactly where she was meant to be. She became that student who always had her hand up in class, always sat at the front and always turned in her assignments early.

One of her professors, Dr. Whitaker, a sharp-eyed woman in her sixties, pulled her aside after a lecture one day. "You remind me of myself when I was your age," she said, studying Emily with curiosity. "Where are you from?"

Emily hesitated. "A little bit of everywhere," she said lightly.

Dr. Whitaker nodded. "Well, wherever it is, you're going to go far. Keep up the good work."

Emily tucked the compliment away, like a rare and precious thing.

To her great surprise, Emily soon found herself in a position she had never imagined—as someone other girls looked up to.

One evening, after class, a girl named Sophia sat next to her in the library, looking hesitant.

"Hey, Emily... can I ask you something?"

Emily closed her laptop. "Sure, what's up?"

Sophia fidgeted. "How do you do it? You always seem so... put together. Like you have everything figured out."

A Candle for Father Joe

Emily let out a short laugh. "Oh, trust me, I don't."

"No, but seriously. You don't get caught up in drama, guys don't mess with you, and you just... know where you're going."

Emily thought for a moment, then shrugged. "I guess... I just know what I want now. And what I don't."

Sophia sighed. "I wish I had that kind of confidence."

Emily smiled, surprising even herself. "Give it time. You'll figure it out."

And just like that, she had accidentally become a role model.

To some extent, she knew her past had something to do with it. She had grown up in fire; she wouldn't fade in the sun.

Weekend Calls

At least once a month, Emily would call Father Joseph, updating him on her life.

"Hey, Father, guess what? I survived the midterms. Barely."

Joseph laughed. "I never had a doubt."

She loved those calls. They made her feel like she had a home to call back to.

And Joseph? He lived for them.

"Do you need anything, Emily?" he asked one evening.

"Father, you've done enough."

"Nonsense," he said. "Remember, I'm your parent. Don't hesitate to ask."

Emily felt something warm in her chest. She had never had anyone say that to her before.

"Thanks, Father. I'll let you know if I need anything."

Before they hung up, he added with a chuckle, "Don't forget to visit your parent sometime."

Emily grinned. "I will, Father. I promise."

The Second Semester

If the first semester had been about adjusting, the second semester was about thriving.

She had aced her classes, impressed her professors, and even earned a small scholarship bonus for academic excellence.

She also got a part-time job at the University, working at the campus bookstore—a humble job that made her feel independent.

"You're turning into a proper adult," Jessica teased.

Emily smirked. "Don't remind me."

But life wasn't all academics. She allowed herself to loosen up—just a little.

She attended student events, joined a study group that somehow turned into a close-knit circle of friends, and even let Jessica drag her to a few parties.

Not that she drank. Or did anything reckless.

She was still Emily—the girl with boundaries, the girl with goals.

But for the first time, she allowed herself to enjoy life.

She even danced once. Only once.

Jessica had nearly fainted in shock.

A Milestone Worth Celebrating

By the time finals came around, Emily had cemented herself as one of the top students in her class. She had never worked so hard for something in her life.

And when the semester ended, and she saw her final grades—a perfect 4.0 GPA—she couldn't believe it.

She called Father Joseph immediately. "Father," she said breathlessly, "I did it. I got straight A's."

Joseph's voice was thick with emotion. "Emily... you made your parent feel proud of you."

For a moment, she couldn't speak.

Then she whispered, "Thanks, Father. That means a lot."

It meant everything.

Chapter 12
The Betrayal

Emily Carter had never been the kind of girl who fell for games. She had been through too much, seen too many cruel things, and spent most of her life expecting the worst from people.

But the University had softened her defenses—she had begun to believe that not everyone had an ulterior motive.

Maybe some people were genuinely kind. That's exactly what she found in Daniel Kingston, who got through her walls.

Daniel was one of those guys who made everything seem effortless. He was smart, funny, and charming—but not in the arrogant way some of the guys were. He had a way of making Emily feel seen, and that was new to her.

It started with study sessions in the library. Then, casual coffee meetups.

Before long, he was texting her every morning, showing up at the bookstore where she worked part-time, and offering to walk her back to her dorm late at night.

For the first time, someone wanted to be around her—

just for her. She felt happy that someone found her company desirable.

"You're different, Emily," Daniel had told her one evening. "You're not like the other girls."

She had scoffed, rolling her eyes. "That's the worst pickup line ever."

But he meant it; she had thought so.

And she let herself feel something for him. Something she had never allowed before.

The Night of Awakening

It was a Friday night, and Emily had been working late at the bookstore when Jessica, her roommate, burst in.

"Emily."

Emily glanced up, immediately catching the panic in Jessica's face. "What's wrong?"

Jessica hesitated. "You need to come with me. Now."

Emily frowned but followed her as they hurried across campus.

Jessica didn't speak, just kept walking fast, gripping Emily's wrist.

And, they entered the dorm common room.

It was packed with students, all gathered around a group of guys laughing loudly. Daniel was in the center of them, beer in hand, leaning back against the couch as his friend patted him on the shoulder.

"You actually pulled it off, man. I can't believe it."

Daniel grinned, shaking his head. "I told you guys, girls like that are the easiest. They pretend to be tough but give them a little attention, and they fall just as hard."

He passed around his cell phone with the selfie he had taken with Emily.

"Look at her smile, man," laughter erupted.

Emily's stomach dropped. Her heart froze.

Jessica whispered, "Emily... I thought you should witness this. That's enough. Come on. Let's go."

But she couldn't move. Because Daniel kept talking.

"I mean, come on. Did you think someone like me would actually be serious about someone like her? How dull life would be?" He smirked. "It was just because of our bet, guys. And I won."

Emily felt the world tilt beneath her feet.

A bet. She had been a joke. The realization hit her like a physical blow.

She wanted to scream, to curse him out, to throw something—but she couldn't.

She just stood there, feeling her entire body go cold.

And then, Daniel saw her. The moment their eyes met, his face drained of color.

"Emily—"

But she didn't wait to hear whatever pathetic excuse he had. She turned and walked away.

She walked away before he could see her cry.

The Spiral

For the whole next week, Emily disappeared from everything. She skipped classes, ignored Jessica's knocks on the door, and buried herself in her bed, feeling broken, humiliated, and completely worthless.

Every time she closed her eyes, she heard his voice—mocking her, laughing at her.

"Girls like her think they are unreachable. But they are the easiest."

She thought she had grown. She thought she had become strong.

But in that moment, she felt like the lost, broken girl she had always been. And worse, she began questioning everything.

Has Father Joseph been wrong about her? Had she ever been worthy of this new life? Has she been fooling herself all along?

An Awakening Call

The call came on a Saturday evening. Her phone had been ringing for days, but she had ignored it.

But something in her chest cracked when she saw Father Joseph's name on the screen. With a shaky breath, she answered.

"Emily." His voice was gentle, warm—concerned.

The moment she heard him, her composure shattered. A single sob escaped her.

"Father," she whispered.

"What happened, child?"

And immediately, she told him everything. Every shameful detail. Every crushing humiliation.

She expected him to be disappointed. To tell her that she should have been more careful, been smarter.

But all he said was: "Emily, listen to me. This does not define you."

She clutched the phone tightly. "But I feel so stupid, Father. I let him in—I trusted him."

"That doesn't make you weak," Joseph said firmly. "It makes you human."

She sniffed. "Then why does it hurt so much?"

"Because you have a heart that longs to be loved," he said

gently. "And Emily—one day, someone will love you for who you are. Not because of a bet. Not because of what they can gain. But because you are worth loving."

Emily closed her eyes, letting his words sink in. She was not broken. She was not worthless.

And she would not let Daniel Kingston take her dignity.

The next morning, Father Joseph made one more call.

To Jim Sullivan.

By the end of the week, the University's Disciplinary Board was involved. With his influence on the Advisory Board, Jim ensured that Daniel Kingston and his friends faced serious consequences.

A formal complaint was filed, and the University took swift action. Daniel was suspended for misconduct.

When Emily walked into class again, her name was no longer whispered in pity—but in admiration. Even the students who had laughed at the bet now looked uncomfortable in her presence as if ashamed.

Some people even began wondering who she really was. After all, the University Board had gotten involved for her.

Some assumed she was the daughter of an influential figure, related to a senator, or a CEO's child.

But Emily didn't correct them. She simply lifted her chin and walked forward, knowing the truth.

She wasn't anyone's daughter. She was just Emily Carter.

And that was enough.

Chapter 13
The Shadow of Accusation

A month later, on a quiet morning, Jim Sullivan's phone rang.

He glanced at the screen. Al Godwin.

Jim's brow furrowed. That was unexpected.

Al was an old friend and Vice President at the University. They had worked together on various projects, but it wasn't often that he called out of the blue.

Jim swiped to answer. "Al, good to hear from you."

But there were no pleasantries.

"Jim, the girl you recommended—Emily Carter—she's in serious trouble."

Jim sat up straighter. A chill crept over him.

"What kind of trouble?"

"She's under investigation for academic dishonesty. Plagiarism was detected in her semester-end paper."

Jim's grip tightened on the phone.

"That doesn't make sense, Al." His voice was calm, but his mind was already racing. "Emily's a girl of integrity. I'd bet my life on it."

Al sighed. "I don't deny that. But the evidence is

stacked against her. Just thought you should know what's happening."

And with that, he hung up.

Jim sat there for a long moment, the phone still in his hand.

Something was very, very wrong.

He decided to call Father Joseph.

The Dean's Office

The moment Emily walked into the Dean's office, she knew something was wrong.

The atmosphere was cold. Sterile. Unforgiving.

Two professors sat across from her, their expressions unreadable.

A disciplinary board member was already present.

And at the head of the table, the Dean himself, Dr. Alden Harper, rested his fingers against his chin, scanning the document in front of him with a grim expression.

Emily's stomach twisted.

"Miss Carter, do you know why you're here?"

The words landed like a hammer.

She swallowed. "No, sir."

"A plagiarism report has been filed against you."

Emily's pulse roared in her ears.

She blinked. "What?"

Dr. Whitman, the professor from her Advanced Ethics class, slid a folder across the table.

Emily's hands trembled as she opened it.

Her final research paper. The one she had spent weeks researching, drafting, and refining.

A bright red note was scrawled across the top:

FLAGGED FOR ACADEMIC DISHONESTY – UNDER INVESTIGATION

Her world tilted.

"Professor, this—this isn't true! I wrote every word myself."

Dr. Whitman's expression was grave. "The system detected significant matches with an online academic database.

We also received an anonymous complaint suggesting you may have had outside assistance in writing your paper."

Emily's breath caught. Anonymous?

Her mind raced, scrambling for logic. How? How could this happen?

And then—a realization hit her like a slap to the face.

Daniel Kingston.

Daniel's Revenge

The whole story reeled fast on the screen of her mind.

Emily had unknowingly made a powerful enemy. Daniel Kingston—the charismatic golden boy of the debate team who had tried to charm his way into her good graces.

When his tactics turned manipulative, Emily had seen through him.

His carefully crafted reputation crumbled.

A two-week suspension. A public humiliation. His perfect image tainted.

From that moment on, Emily could feel it.

The way his eyes lingered just a little too long when she walked past. The easy grin that never quite reached his eyes. An undercurrent of something dark was beneath his polished exterior.

She knew he wanted payback.

And now, he had found the perfect way to get it.

She knew it was him.

She just couldn't prove it.

Falling Apart

Emily tried to defend herself, but the board was unmoved.

"Miss Carter, we take academic dishonesty very seriously. If the investigation confirms misconduct, it could result in permanent expulsion."

Her stomach lurched. Everything she had worked for—her scholarship, her degree, her future—was on the line.

"But I didn't do this," she pleaded. "You have to believe me."

Dr. Whitman hesitated. There was something in her voice—something real, something raw.

But the Dean remained firm. "A thorough investigation will be conducted. Until then, your scholarship and enrollment are placed on hold."

Emily stumbled out of the office, barely making it outside before the tears choked her throat.

The fear was overwhelming.

She was alone. No family to support her. No one to turn to, except Father Joseph.

How often could she bother him, especially now, with this kind of case?

She thought the system had always been against people like her.

She felt like that orphaned child again.

Unwanted. Disposable. Forgotten.

The Call That Changed Everything

Emily didn't know where else to turn.

But there was one number she had memorized by heart.

She dialed.

"Father?" Her voice broke.

A Candle for Father Joe

On the other end, Father Joseph's calm, steady voice filled the silence. "Emily, what's wrong?"

And just like that, the floodgates opened.

She told him everything—her voice shaking, her heart sinking.

When she finished, there was a long pause.

Then, in the gentlest voice, he said: "You are not alone. And you will not let this define you."

Emily closed her eyes, letting his words anchor her.

"Fight back," he told her. "You didn't come this far just to let someone like that boy take everything away from you."

She nodded, wiping her tears. "But how?"

"You have people who believe in you, Emily. And so do I."

Chapter 14
The Reckoning

Emily sat alone in her dorm room, staring blankly at the unopened textbook on her desk. How had everything fallen apart so fast?

She had worked so hard. Sacrificed so much.

And now, it all felt like it was slipping through her fingers.

Her scholarship.

Her future.

Her dignity.

Would they ever believe her? Would she even get the chance to prove her innocence?

Emily didn't know that the storm had already begun to turn in a different direction.

Jim Sullivan sat in his office, his phone pressed against his ear, his expression sharp.

He had heard enough.

The moment he hung up with Father Joseph, he made a call.

Al Godwin answered almost immediately.

"Al," Jim's voice was firm, "that girl Emily Carter wouldn't cheat if her life depended on it."

The VP hesitated. "The evidence is pretty damning, Jim."

Jim's voice darkened. "Then you need to dig deeper. Because something isn't right."

Al exhaled. Jim's reputation carried weight.

"Alright," Al finally said. "I'll push for a thorough investigation. But if nothing turns up—"

"It will," Jim cut in. "And when it does, I want you to remember this conversation."

Within days, the University's IT department launched a forensic investigation into Emily's paper.

What they found shocked them.

The Truth Stranger than ......

Emily sat in the dimly lit office, her pulse pounding. Across from her sat Dr. Evelyn Johnson, the University's lead Cybersecurity Specialist.

A no-nonsense woman, Dr. Johnson had the air of someone who had seen it all—and didn't waste time on nonsense.

She slid a laptop toward Emily.

"Miss Carter, I need you to take a look at something."

Emily stiffened as she glanced at the screen.

It was an email.

The subject line:

URGENT: SECURITY UPDATE REQUIRED

Emily's stomach dropped. She remembered that email. She had received it two weeks ago.

The message had read:

Dear Student,

Due to a recent security breach, we require all students to reset their login credentials to prevent unauthorized access. Please update your password using the secure link below. Failure to do so may result in loss of account access.

The sender's address looked official.

The website looked identical to the university portal.

And she had entered her password without a second thought.

Dr. Johnson exhaled. "Emily, do you remember this email?"

Emily's throat was dry. "Yes, and I responded promptly."

Dr. Johnson nodded gravely. "Well, you didn't do anything wrong. You were targeted."

Emily's breath hitched. "Daniel?"

Dr. Johnson's lips tightened. "Yes. And here's how we know."

She turned the laptop toward Emily.

A list of login timestamps appeared on the screen.

Emily's account had been accessed from an off-campus IP address—at 2:43 AM—the night before the plagiarism report was filed.

Emily's voice shook. "I was asleep."

Dr. Johnson clicked again.

A list of locations appeared.

One of them?

A student apartment complex just a block from campus.

Daniel Kingston's building.

Emily felt a surge of anger.

She had thought she was fighting a system that didn't care.

Instead, she had been stabbed in the back.

By a man who wanted nothing more than to see her fall.

Dr. Johnson leaned back, crossing her arms. "We also found a duplicate of your paper uploaded to the online academic database—by an anonymous user."

Emily's breath hitched. "He set me up."

Dr. Johnson nodded grimly. "And now we have the proof."

Daniel's Downfall

The next day, Daniel Kingston's smug world came crashing down.

Emily sat beside Jim Sullivan in the Dean's office as the University Board reviewed the final findings.

The Vice President of the University spoke, his voice icy. "Mr. Kingston, we have substantial evidence that you illegally accessed another student's account and falsified documents to frame her for academic dishonesty."

Daniel's cocky expression vanished.

The VP continued, "This is not just a violation of the University's Honor Code. It is a criminal act."

Daniel's hands clenched into pale fists. "I don't know what you're talking about."

"Here is the evidence," VP turned his laptop for Daniel to see.

Daniel's face darkened.

He had lost. Expelled.

Permanently barred from the University.

Emily breathed for the first time in days.

"Al, Emily Carter is a young woman of integrity, as I told you before. I am glad the truth is now right in front of you. And... thank you for initiating the new investigation."

. . .

Standing Tall

When Emily returned to the Dean's office a week later, it was on her own terms.

She wasn't the scared girl from before. She sat tall, listened as she apologized, and accepted her reinstatement.

But before leaving, she turned to Dr. Harper.

Her voice was steady, unwavering. "You treated me like I was guilty before even giving me a chance. You wouldn't have done that if I had the right last name."

The Dean had no words.

Emily didn't wait for them.

She walked out with her head held high.

Chapter 15
The Best Summer Ever

On a busy morning at the Outreach Center, Father Joseph sat down for a moment after spending a few hours helping out. He didn't feel well.

He knew it was coming.

The fatigue had been creeping in slowly—at first, just a lingering exhaustion after long days at the Center. But now, it had grown into something more—a heaviness in his chest, a deep weariness that wouldn't leave, especially when climbing the stairs to his apartment.

Joseph had never been one to worry about his health. He had endured health struggles in seminary, sleepless nights during pastoral emergencies, and years of self-sacrifice. He was a man used to giving, not receiving.

But this was different. The doctor's words had hung over him like an unshakable weight.

"Your heart is weak. It's not pumping enough blood."

"Maybe a complication from the COVID-19 vaccination you had a few years ago."

"Surgery is the only solution."

Joseph said simply shaking his head, "I've lived long enough, doctor. I have no regrets. I will just go on like this, for as long as I can."

The doctor sighed, clearly frustrated but not entirely surprised.

"At least let me increase your medication. But you know, Father..." he said, "sometimes you need to obey your doctor."

Joseph just smiled at that.

The Best Summer of Their Lives

Emily got a short summer break and came home.

She didn't check into a hotel. She didn't stay with friends.

She came straight to Father Joseph's apartment—

For the first time, she called it *home*.

The moment she stepped inside, she threw her arms around him in a tight hug, something she rarely did.

"Oh, Father, I missed you!" she beamed.

Joseph chuckled, patting her back. "Well, you didn't forget your old parent after all."

She pulled back and smirked. "How could I? Who else would keep me in check?"

She looked around the apartment and breathed in. "Do you buy fresh flowers every day, Father?"

"Why?" Joseph asked, genuinely curious.

"It smells fresh in here... like walking into a garden in bloom," she said with a smile.

Joseph laughed. "Don't be silly, young lady."

But as she wandered further in, brushing her fingers over the back of the chair and glancing at the books stacked near the window, Joseph felt a quiet ache stir in his chest.

He remembered the first time she had come here.

Timid. Thin. Eyes shadowed by too many hard years.

She had sat stiffly at the edge of the armchair like she didn't belong, afraid even to touch the glass of water he gave her.

Now, here she was—radiant, self-assured, laughing in his kitchen.

She even teased him about the flowers.

She was different now, Joseph thought—her confidence was solid, her smile brighter.

But she was still Emily.

And Joseph loved her like the daughter he never had.

"Alright," she said, clapping her hands together. "What are we eating?"

Joseph raised an eyebrow. "We?"

She grinned. "Yes, *we*. I'm not letting you survive on canned soup and toast this whole week."

"Excuse me, my cooking has improved dramatically," he said with mock offense, walking toward the tiny kitchen. "I now make three types of eggs."

Emily burst out laughing. "Perfect. I'll handle everything else."

They moved around the kitchen in an easy rhythm. She chopped vegetables with confident hands. He stirred a pot of rice, humming an old tune under his breath. Occasionally, their arms would bump or they'd reach for the same utensil, both smiling in quiet amusement.

As the aromas filled the apartment—ginger, garlic, and chopped chicken pieces—something gently frying. Emily opened the cabinet.

"You still keep your tea in that old biscuit tin?" she asked, pulling it down.

"Some traditions are sacred," Joseph said, pouring water into the kettle.

Soon, they were sitting at the small kitchen table, sipping tea and eating a simple dinner they had made together.

The lamplight softened the room, catching the edges of the rosary beads near the window, and the fresh flowers in the jar on the table leaned slightly toward them, as if listening.

For a moment, there were no regrets, no memories that hurt, no fears of the future.

Just a priest and a young woman sharing a quiet evening.

Just a father and a daughter, healing in the warmth of ordinary things.

They lingered over their tea long after the plates were cleared. It was something different in Joseph's life, sitting in the kitchen with someone so close to his life.

Emily didn't feel rushed to get up either.

Heart to Heart

The window was open just a crack, and the soft hush of summer air drifted in. Outside, the streetlight flickered to life. Inside, silence fell—not awkward, but restful.

Emily tapped her spoon against the edge of her mug.

"You know," she said slowly, "when I was little, I used to imagine someone like you."

Joseph looked up, surprised.

"Not *you*, exactly," she added with a crooked smile. "But someone who actually saw me. Someone who didn't just walk past. Someone who cared."

Joseph's voice was quiet. "I'm sorry it took me so long."

She shook her head. "You found me when I needed it most. And not just once."

He swallowed gently. "There were so many days I wished I had done more. So many nights I prayed for another chance."

Emily looked down at her tea, then back at him.

"Well, you got one."

They smiled at each other, and the silence returned—now fuller, richer.

After a while, she reached across the table, fingers brushing the side of his hand.

"I think I like it here," she said. "The flowers. The smell of books. Even your scary bookshelf of theology."

Joseph chuckled. "Scary? That shelf is a treasure."

She grinned. "Then maybe I'll stay for a while and organize it."

He raised an eyebrow. "That would be heresy."

They both laughed, and for a moment, it felt like they had always shared this kitchen, this life, this belonging.

Outside, a breeze rustled the leaves.

Inside, something had settled.

Not every story needs a grand miracle.

Sometimes, grace comes like this—

Quiet as tea cooling in a cup.

Steady as a heart that still remembers how to hope.

* * *

For one glorious week, life felt... normal.

She took him out to dinner, playfully insisting that he had to experience "student-style dining" at her favorite café.

She helped him cook, teasing him about his lack of kitchen skills.

She sat with him on the balcony, sipping tea and talking about her classes, her dreams, and the world she was discovering.

She was thriving, and he had the chance to see it. That was enough.

But, he knew, the joy was fleeting because his body was failing him faster than he let on.

The Hidden Struggle

One evening, they visited Jim and Mary Sullivan. Jim greeted them warmly, pulling Emily into a playful hug.

"Are they treating you well over there at the University?" he asked.

Emily smirked. "Oh, sure. The boys are now scared to even talk to me."

They all laughed, enjoying an evening of lighthearted conversation over tea and cookies.

But on the way back, as they climbed the stairs to the apartment, Emily noticed something — Joseph's breathing was heavy.

"Father?" she asked, stopping on the step above him.

"Oh, just tired," he brushed it off with a wave of his hand.

But she didn't miss how his hand trembled slightly as he reached for the railing.

She hesitated for a moment. Should she let Jim know?

A Morning of Concern

A Candle for Father Joe

The next morning, Emily rose early, expecting to find the kitchen humming with the familiar sounds of Father Joseph—boiling water for tea, shuffling his old slippers, humming an off-key hymn as he prepared to head to the Outreach Center.

But the apartment was silent.

She walked to his door, her brow furrowed.

"Father?" she called softly. No answer.

She hesitated, then turned the handle and slowly pushed the door open.

He was still in bed. Not reading. Not praying. Just lying still, his face too pale, his breath slower than usual. His Bible lay untouched on the nightstand.

Emily's heart clenched.

"You're never this late to wake up," she said, sitting carefully at the edge of the bed. "Are you okay?"

He opened his eyes and offered her a faint smile—gentle, but tired.

"Maybe my body's finally realized it's not twenty-five anymore."

"That's not funny," she said, trying to laugh it off. But her voice betrayed her.

"Do you want me to call the doctor?"

"It's nothing, girl. I've seen him already," Joseph replied lightly. "He says I'm perfect."

Emily gave him a look. "Perfect? That means either you're lying or your doctor's blind."

He chuckled softly. "Probably both."

But she saw it—the subtle tremor in his hands as he reached for his glasses, the heaviness in his limbs, the way his smile lingered just a second too long to mask the weariness underneath.

Joseph turned to Emily with the same weak smile, "At my age, this is normal."

She didn't press.

She wanted to believe him. She needed to believe him.

She prayed, he was right.

Chapter 16
A Goodbye that Felt Different

The next day, she packed her small suitcase for her summer job at the university. They didn't talk much that morning—just moved around each other in a quiet rhythm.

But when she reached the door, something inside her resisted.

She turned back and walked straight into his arms.

"Promise me, you'll take care of yourself," she said softly, holding him tighter than usual.

Joseph laid a hand on her head like a blessing. "I will. You know me—I've always been good at doing nothing."

She laughed through her worry. "That's a lie. You don't even sit down for tea unless someone makes you."

He kissed her on the forehead. "You always did know how to get the truth out of me."

She pulled back but didn't let go of his hands.

"I'll be fine, girl. Don't worry about me," he held her hand tight.

She rolled her eyes but smiled. "I always worry about you."

Then, as she walked toward the door, she turned back, giving him a long look.

"I'll visit again soon," she said, her voice lower now, almost a whisper.

"I'll be here," Joseph replied, but his voice wavered ever so slightly. "Waiting."

She nodded. Then paused.

One last look.

The hallway light framed him like a painting—his kind eyes, the lines on his face, the quiet dignity of a man who had given everything and now had so little left to give.

"Don't forget to answer your phone, old man," she said, forcing a smile.

"I wouldn't dare," he said, smiling back.

She turned and walked down the stairs, each step feeling heavier than the last.

At the bottom, she paused and looked up.

He was still there, standing in the doorway, his hand raised in farewell.

She waved once more. "Bye, Father."

Joseph watched her disappear from view.

And when the door finally closed behind him, he leaned against the frame, pressing a hand to his chest.

He didn't know how much time he had left.

But he knew what little remained, he would spend finishing what he had begun—for her.

And for the daughter he had once failed to save.

And he also knew how a father's heart aches when he fears he might not get another chance to say goodbye.

The Doctor's Warning

A few days later, Joseph returned to the doctor.

A Candle for Father Joe

The fatigue was worsening. He had almost fainted at Mass, gripping the altar to steady himself.

Seated on the edge of the examination table, he watched as the doctor studied the latest cardiogram, his brow furrowing with concern.

"Father," the doctor said at last, his voice heavy but respectful, "your heart is deteriorating—fast. I'll tell you again... surgery is the only real option."

Joseph looked down at his hands—tired, worn thin from years of ministry and service.

He drew in a breath. "And if I don't?" he asked quietly.

The doctor set the chart aside and met his eyes with a gentleness that masked nothing.

"Then we'll continue with medication. It might buy you some time. But that's all I can promise."

Joseph nodded slowly, almost to himself, as if accepting an answer he already knew was coming.

"Then... let's do that," he said, in a voice calm but hollow.

The doctor hesitated. "You know how this ends, Father."

Joseph smiled faintly. "I know."

The doctor studied him for a long moment. Then looking upward, he said softly, "And so Father, as you are more aware than me... it's all in His hands now."

Joseph's gaze drifted toward the window, where fading sunlight streamed through the glass like a final blessing.

He exhaled slowly. "Yes," he said. "It always has been."

But in the quiet that followed, something inside him stirred—a weight not of fear, but of unfinished grace.

He looked back at the doctor. "Just... keep me going a little longer," he said gently. "There's something I need to finish."

Joseph rose from the seat, slower than usual, shoulders

slightly slumped—not from weakness, but from the burden of what still remained undone.

He hoped the doctor would buy time long enough for him to finish it.

The Unfinished Business

Joseph returned to his quiet apartment, sitting in his chair and staring at the fading evening light.

He had lived his life in service. He had shepherded his people well. He was ready to go.

There was only one thing left to do.

Catherine. Emily's mother.

The woman he had failed all those years ago. He had to find her.

To give Emily back to her mother. And to give Catherine the daughter she had lost.

Only then, he thought, could his soul depart in peace.

He let out a long, shaky breath.

"I have fought the good fight... I have run the race... I have kept the faith."

But...... before the final call, there was one last lap of the race left to run.

A deep sigh escaped his throat.

Chapter 17
The Search for Catherine

Joseph's first prayer after his Mass the next morning was —

"Dear Lord, you have carried me through a life of sacraments, of sorrow, and of service. I tried to be faithful to my call and showed your love to Your people.

If I have ever found favor in Your eyes, grant me this:

Let me give that girl back to her mother.

Let me give that mother her child.

And if I cannot live long enough to see it happen...

Then let the path I lay be clear enough for them to find each other." Amen.

The thought had been haunting Father Joseph ever since Emily left.

Find Catherine.

Joseph sat in his small apartment, staring at the faded photograph in his hands—the only image he had of Catherine with the baby from when she lived in the small apartment Jim Sullivan had arranged for her nearly two decades ago.

Where had she gone after that?

How had she survived?

Was she still alive?

His first call was to Jim Sullivan. Jim didn't hesitate. "We'll find her, Father. I have a few contacts. Let's start with them."

And so began the search.

He started with Law Enforcement & Private Detectives.

With his connections, Jim reached out to a retired detective from the PD, John Smith.

"You're looking for a woman who disappeared nearly twenty years ago?" the detective asked, raising an eyebrow.

Jim nodded. "A young mother, abandoned, with no support, trying to make it on her own. Any records—employment, rental history, anything?"

The detective sighed. "It's hard without a paper trail. Women in those situations don't always leave footprints. But I'll see what I can do."

They relentlessly went on with online searches and checked Databases.

Despite lacking technological skills, Joseph spent long hours at the Outreach Center computer, going through missing person databases, homeless shelter registries, and social media platforms.

Nothing.

The more he looked, the more he feared the worst.

Detective Smith reached out to Women's Shelters & Support Centers.

Jim and Mary contacted women's advocacy groups, local shelters and crisis centers.

A few places recognized her name but said she hadn't been there in years.

"She was here briefly," one shelter manager said, "but she moved on."

It was a trail gone cold. Every lead ended in disappointment.

And with each dead end, Joseph felt the weight of time pressing harder on him. His rest outdid his working hours. He drank more cups of coffee than ever in his life to keep him alert and continue his online searches.

A Breakthrough

Months had gone by without any promising leads to Catherine. They were almost at the point of giving up.

Just when hope was fading, Jim's phone rang.

It was Detective Smith.

"I think I found her."

Jim's heart leaped. "Where?"

"She's working as a waitress at a hotel downtown. Living in a low-cost apartment complex nearby. Name is still Catherine Carter."

Jim wasted no time. He picked up the phone and called the hotel, asking to speak with Catherine Carter.

Moments later, her voice came through the line—cautious, tired, yet unmistakable.

"This is Catherine."

Jim took a deep breath. "Catherine, my name is Jim Sullivan. I'm a friend of Father Joseph."

Silence.

Then, a sharp, clipped response: "I have nothing to do with him. I have nothing to do with the Church."

The line went dead.

Jim stared at the phone. "Well," he muttered. "That went well."

Mary placed a gentle hand on his arm. "Let's try again. A different way. In person, this time."

Jim sighed, rubbing his temple. "She doesn't want to be found, Mary."

Mary met his eyes, her expression determined. "That doesn't mean she doesn't need to be."

A Woman-to-Woman Conversation

That Saturday afternoon, Jim and Mary drove to Catherine's apartment.

They had no appointment, no guarantee she'd even open the door. But they had one shot.

Mary knocked. After a long pause, the door creaked open.

Catherine stood there, her expression unreadable, her eyes weary, as if life had taken more from her than it ever gave.

"I don't do charity," she said flatly, eyeing Mary's polished look.

Mary smiled. "I'm not here for that. I'm studying the working conditions of women in hospitality. Would you mind if I asked you a few questions?"

Catherine hesitated. Finally, she sighed. "Fine. Five minutes."

She let them in.

The apartment was small, sparsely furnished, but spotless.

She lived —a woman who had fought for every inch of her dignity.

Mary sat across from her, offering warmth without pity. "So, how long have you been working at the hotel?"

"Few years," Catherine said vaguely.

"Must be tough." Mary's voice was kind.

Catherine shrugged. "Pays the bills."

Mary smiled. "You have family?"

Something shifted in Catherine's face.

"Had," she said, her voice hollow.

Mary leaned forward slightly. "Your daughter?"

Catherine froze. Her hands tightened around her coffee cup.

"Why are you really here?" she asked, her voice colder now.

Mary exhaled softly. "Because she's alive. And I can help you find her."

Catherine's breath hitched. For a moment, her mask cracked.

But then, she shook her head. "No. That's impossible."

"It's not," Mary said gently. "She's in college now. A smart, strong young woman. She's done well. Don't you want to see her?"

Catherine let out a shaky breath, looking away.

"I never wanted to give her up," she whispered. "I fought... I fought so hard. But they forced me. My parents. The family. No one cared what I wanted."

Tears glistened in her eyes, but she blinked them away.

Mary reached across the table, her voice soft but firm.

"Then let's make it happen right now."

Catherine stared at her, something breaking inside her.

"But... why now? After all these years?"

Mary hesitated, then spoke the truth.

"Because Father Joseph doesn't have much time left."

Catherine stiffened. "He's sick?"

Mary nodded. "And old. He is no more the young priest you had met.... Before he goes, he wants to give you back what you have lost. He wants to make things right."

Catherine let out a shaky laugh. "Make things right? You think he can undo twenty years of my loss, my pain?"

Mary held her gaze. "Maybe not. But maybe he can give you your daughter back."

Silence.

Catherine swallowed hard. "If I meet her," she said slowly, "I don't want her to know everything. Not yet."

"That's your decision," Mary assured her. "But one step at a time. Will you meet with Father Joseph?"

Catherine was silent for a long time.

"Remember, he came running to that motel when you needed him most...He went to the hospital to find out how you were doing... He also arranged an apartment for you to stay when you had nowhere to go."

A sudden sobbing came out of her.

"Catherine, you are mad at him for not doing what he couldn't do." Mary's voice cracked a little.

Finally, Catherine exhaled and nodded.

"I'll think about it."

Mary reached out and gently squeezed her hand.

"That's all we ask. And that too, only if you want to get your daughter back."

In slow strides, Mary left the apartment.

Chapter 18
A Shepherd's Burden

When Father Joseph learned Catherine was still alive, something inside him stirred with hope.

For twenty years, he had carried the weight of unfinished business, the silent regret that had lingered in the deepest corners of his heart.

Now, the end was in sight. He had found Catherine. He had found Emily.

And if he could bring them together—if he could give them back to each other—then, maybe he could finally leave this world in peace.

But his body was failing him faster than he had expected. The countless hours of sleepless nights, pouring over online searches, making phone calls, and pushing himself beyond his limits had taken their toll.

The fatigue was getting worse. The dizziness more frequent. Even the smallest tasks left him breathless.

The day after Jim and Mary met Catherine, Joseph woke up and found he could barely stand. He reached for his phone, his fingers trembling.

"Jim," he whispered when the call connected. "I need help."

The Emergency Room

Jim and Mary arrived within minutes.

Joseph sat in his chair, looking far smaller than the man they had known for years. His skin was pale, his breath labored, his once steady hands weak and unsteady.

Jim sat beside him, his voice laced with concern. "Father, why didn't you call us sooner?"

Joseph smiled faintly. "I thought I could hold on. But I guess... I was wrong."

Mary placed a gentle hand on his shoulder. "We're taking you to the hospital. No arguments."

He didn't fight them. He didn't have the strength to.

The ambulance arrived too quickly, yet too slowly. As the paramedics lifted him onto the stretcher, Joseph exhaled deeply, as though releasing a burden only he could feel.

His voice was barely a whisper. "Take care of Emily."

Jim gripped his hand. "We will, Father."

"Don't tell her anything about me now. She has exams all this week."

"Yes, Father. But first, let's take care of you."

Joseph closed his eyes.

For the first time he could remember, he let someone else carry him.

The beeping of monitors. The muffled voices of nurses. The cold touch of an IV.

Joseph drifted in and out of consciousness, caught

between the present and the past. He heard voices that weren't there.

"Father... Don't you want to see me get a nice job, a house, and a great family of my own, as you said when you coaxed me into accepting your challenge?"

"I'm going to challenge you. Live up to your promise."

"I will drag you to my graduation, old man. No excuses of bad health."

"I will then take you to my home, not anymore in that tiny apartment."

Emily's laughter echoed in his ears. "My children need a grandfather."

"Bye, my parent."

He wanted to respond, wanted to assure her that he was still there for her.

But his body had other plans.

The Doctor's Verdict

Jim and Mary sat in the hospital room, watching as Joseph's breathing evened out slightly.

A doctor entered, his expression professional but heavy with unspoken words.

"His heart is weak," the doctor said, flipping through Joseph's chart. "We've stabilized him, but without surgery... there's not much we can do."

Jim frowned. "He's refused surgery before."

The doctor nodded. "And he's refusing it now."

Mary inhaled sharply. "Then what's next?"

The doctor sighed. "Make him comfortable. Ensure he gets good nursing care. He has very little time left—weeks, maybe days. We'll keep him here until he's stable enough to be moved."

Jim swallowed hard. He had always known Joseph was nearing the end.

But hearing it spoken aloud made it real....Too real.

Nursing Home

A week later, when Joseph was stable enough, Jim and Mary—along with a few other parishioners—made arrangements to move him to a peaceful, well-staffed nursing home.

It wasn't a hospital but the best care he could have without medical intervention. As they wheeled him into the new room, Joseph gave them a tired but grateful smile.

"I never thought I'd end up in a place like this," he mused, looking around.

Jim smirked. "Yeah, well, you didn't leave us much of a choice."

Mary adjusted the blankets over him. "You need rest, Father. No more running around trying to save the world."

Joseph chuckled weakly. "But I have one last mission left."

Jim and Mary exchanged a glance.

They knew what he meant.

Catherine and Emily.

Mary took his hand. "Rest first. We'll take care of the rest."

Joseph nodded. For now, that was enough.

But he knew, he was running out of time.

Chapter 19
A Fading Light

A few days later, at Jim's house, the phone rang.

Jim answered. "Emily, good to hear your voice! What's up?"

"I tried calling Father a few times, but he didn't answer," Emily said, her voice filled with concern. "I was wondering where he was."

Jim hesitated before replying. "Emily... his health has been declining. He couldn't take care of everything anymore, so we moved him to a nursing home."

"To a nursing home?" A pause. Then— "Is he okay?"

Jim forced a reassuring tone. "He's in good hands. He's getting proper meals, and some exercise. He's safe, Emily."

There was a long silence on the other end.

Then came her voice. "Jim, it's my graduation next Saturday. I want all of you to come. That's why I called Father. Can I have his contact number?"

Jim paused, debating. Would Joseph want her to see him like this? Would she be able to handle it?

After a moment, he relented. He gave her the number.

She hung up and immediately dialed the nursing home.

. . .

The phone rang in Joseph's room.

A nurse picked it up and then gently placed it in his hand.

"Hi, Father, how are you?"

Joseph gathered all his strength to sound normal. "Oh, I'm fine," he said, forcing lightness into his voice. "They want to spoil me here. Now I don't have to cook, do dishes—not even make my bed!"

Emily didn't buy it. "But they won't let you go out, will they?"

Joseph chuckled. "No, they won't. Apparently, I'm too valuable to be wandering around."

She hesitated. "Next Saturday is my graduation, Father. You are the only parent I want at my big event."

Joseph felt his throat tighten. "I will try, Emily. If they let me travel, I'll be there. Otherwise, Jim and Mary will take pictures and show them to me."

A long pause.

"That's not the same, Father." Her voice was softer now. "But I don't want you to take the risk and get worse."

Joseph exhaled. "You are my kind of girl."

Emily sighed. "Okay, Father. I'll fly down to you early next morning with my diploma. I need your blessing."

Joseph felt his heart ache. "We will have a great Graduation Party here," he said.

She laughed lightly. "More importantly, I want to spend time with you."

Another pause.

"Bye, Father Joe. See you soon."

Joseph closed his eyes.

"Goodbye, my girl."

He held the phone in his weak hands, listening to the soft click as she hung up.

He felt his entire body grow heavier. A deep exhaustion settled over him.

And he knew.

He wouldn't make it to Saturday.

The Last Letter

The next day, Joseph felt he had better strength. He sat up on his chair.

There was one last thing left to do.

He took out his worn leather journal—the one where he had poured his prayers, his confessions, and his deepest regrets. With a shaky hand, he pulled out a blank sheet of paper and began writing.

He wrote everything.

About Catherine. About Emily. About the impossible choice he had been forced to make. About the burden he had carried in silence.

By the time he finished, his hands were trembling, his breath shallow.

He folded the letter carefully, sealed it in an envelope, and wrote Emily's name on it.

Then, with a deep sigh, he placed it inside the journal, resting his hand over it for a long moment.

Now, she would know. Now, she would understand.

A small smile formed on his lips as he whispered, "Lord, now You may dismiss Your servant in peace."

And that night, for the first time in a long, long time, he slept without pain.

. . .

The Last Rites

The days and nights blurred together, his body growing weaker, frailer.

By Thursday, he could barely sit up. The pain in his chest grew sharper, his breathing more labored.

He knew what was coming.

So he called Father Michael, the parish pastor.

"I need you to give me the Last Rites," he said, his voice barely above a whisper.

Father Michael arrived quickly, kneeling beside him.

With trembling hands, Joseph made the Sign of the Cross.

Father Michael placed his hand on Joseph's forehead, whispering the familiar words:

"Through this holy anointing, may the Lord in His love and mercy help you with the grace of the Holy Spirit."

Joseph exhaled, a wave of calm settling over him. "Amen."

"May the Lord who frees you from sin save you and raise you up."

His eyes fluttered shut. "Amen."

He barely registered Father Michael placing the Eucharist on his tongue.

"The Body of Christ."

"Amen," Joseph whispered.

And then, he was alone again.

His breathing was slow, his body too heavy to move.

But his heart...

His heart was at peace.

Graduation Day

Saturday morning arrived.

Joseph barely opened his eyes.

Jim and Mary stopped by before heading to the graduation ceremony.

They found him asleep, his chest rising and falling in slow, shallow breaths.

They didn't want to wake him.

So they sat beside him for a few moments, whispered a prayer for him, and left silently.

The Precious Moments

The caretaker sat nearby, watching him.

Slowly, Joseph's breathing grew softer.

More shallow.

A moment passed. Then another.

The caretaker saw the shift.

Something was changing.

She immediately picked up the phone and dialed Father Michael.

"He's going," she whispered.

Within minutes, Father Michael arrived.

He sat beside Joseph's bedside, taking his cold, frail hand in his own.

He whispered the prayers for the dying.

"Go forth, Christian soul, from this world... may you live in peace this day, may your home be with God in Zion, with Mary, the Virgin Mother of God, with Joseph, and all the angels and saints."

Joseph's breathing hitched.

A final, shallow exhale.

Then, nothing.

A stillness settled over the room.

Father Michael lowered his head.

"Eternal rest grant unto him, O Lord, and let perpetual light shine upon him."

He reached over, gently closing Joseph's eyes. "May he Rest in Peace."

The shepherd had gone home.

Chapter 20
The Evening Rain

The night after Father Joseph's funeral, a heavy rainstorm swept through the town. The streets shimmered under streetlights, the downpour creating a rhythmic symphony against the pavement.

Inside the rectory, Father Michael sat at his desk, staring at the flickering candle before him. The day had been long. The church had been filled to capacity, the pews crowded with mourners who came to bid farewell to a man who had lived only for others.

But as the night deepened, something stirred in him—a sense of unease, a quiet call to step outside.

He grabbed an umbrella and stepped into the rain. The wind was cold, the water soaking into his shoes, but he barely noticed. His eyes were drawn toward the grotto of the Virgin Mary, where a lone figure stood, motionless.

A young woman, drenched in the downpour, her gaze locked onto the statue as if searching for answers in the silent stone.

He recognized her.

She had been there at the funeral, sitting quietly with Jim and Mary Sullivan.

Carefully, Father Michael approached, the rain beating against the fabric of his umbrella.

She didn't move or acknowledge him, until he was just a few feet away.

"You'll catch a cold out here," he said gently.

She hesitated, then finally turned her face toward him. The streaks of rain mingled with unseen tears.

"He was everything to me," she whispered, her voice nearly lost in the storm.

Father Michael's brows furrowed. "Who?"

"Father Joe," she answered, her words almost drowned in the heavy rain.

The weight of those words pressed into his heart.

"You knew him well?" he asked, though he already knew the answer.

She swallowed hard, then nodded. "He was my parent."

Father Michael felt a pang of sorrow. He had known Joseph for years, yet here was a part of his life he had never fully understood.

"Who are you?"

She looked at him, her eyes filled with an emotion he couldn't quite place.

"Emily Carter."

And just like that, she turned and walked away, the rain swallowing her into the night.

Father Michael stood there for a long time, watching her disappear.

Searching for Emily

As soon as he went back inside, he called Jim Sullivan.

"Jim, I just saw a young woman standing in the rain by the grotto."

Jim's voice on the other end was tense. "Describe her."

"Dark hair, about twenty, soaking wet, looked heartbroken. She called herself Emily Carter."

Jim froze. He turned to Mary, who was sitting beside him.

"Did you say she was walking in the rain?" he asked.

"Yes. She walked away before I could say anything else."

Jim sighed, rubbing his forehead. "Let me see if I can find her."

He hung up and turned to Mary.

"Where would she go?"

Mary's face softened. "Jim... she may have gone to Father's apartment."

They didn't hesitate. Grabbing their coats, they rushed to Joseph's small apartment.

As soon as they pulled up, they saw light inside.

The door was slightly ajar.

Jim pushed it open.

Inside, Emily sat on the floor, soaked to the skin, her hair damp and tangled. The apartment was dimly lit, the only illumination was from a small lamp on the side table.

She didn't move.

She barely even blinked.

Her expression was empty, but her eyes told a different story.

A story of devastation.

The Weight of Loss

Emily's mind kept replaying what had happened just two days ago.

Her graduation.

The day she had waited for, worked so hard for.

Her only disappointment was that her "parent" couldn't be there to witness it.

She had stepped out of the stage with pride, her diploma in hand, ready to prove that she had made it. That she had overcome.

And then Jim approached her.

His face was grave. Too grave.

"Emily... Father Joseph is gone."

The world tilted beneath her.

Her diploma suddenly felt like a piece of paper.

Her achievements suddenly felt meaningless.

She cried aloud, not caring about the hundreds of people watching, or the whispers or the pitying looks.

She told Jim she wanted to leave immediately with them.

She arrived at his apartment, his home, her home.

She entered his empty room.

The bed was neatly made.

The rosary he always prayed with sat untouched on the nightstand.

She knelt beside his bed, pressing her forehead against the mattress, and for the first time, prayed with real fervor.

Now, sitting in the same apartment after his funeral, she felt nothing.

No more tears.

No more pain.

Just numbness.

Like floating in a cloud of solidified sorrow.

A Hand to Hold

Mary walked in slowly, kneeling beside her.

She gently took Emily's cold hands in hers, raising her up with quiet tenderness.

"Come, child," she whispered. "Let's get you warm."

Emily didn't resist.

She let Mary guide her to the small bedroom and hand her a clean, dry dress.

Minutes later, Emily reappeared in a simple dress, her wet hair combed back, but her eyes still void of light.

Mary sat beside her on the sofa.

"Emily, you need rest. Come home with us."

Emily shook her head, her voice barely a whisper. "No... I'll stay here. This is my Father's place."

Jim and Mary exchanged glances.

Mary touched Emily's shoulder. "Alright, sweetheart. We'll see you tomorrow."

Jim sighed, placing a hand on Emily's back.

"Get some sleep," he murmured. "Tomorrow is a long day."

Emily didn't answer.

She just sat there, staring into nothing.

* * *

The Letter

The following morning, Father Michael and Jim arrived at the nursing home.

They had come to collect Joseph's few belongings and move them to the apartment.

Mary had stayed behind with Emily, bringing a tray of warm breakfast.

"The girl needs to eat," she had told Jim before he left.

At the nursing home, they had carefully packed Joseph's

few possessions in a bag: A few clothes, his rosary, some personal effects.

And then, Father Michael found his journal.

It sat neatly on the table as if waiting for them.

As he picked it up, a small envelope slipped out.

It was sealed and addressed in Joseph's familiar handwriting.

To Emily.

Jim and Father Michael stared at each other.

"This is it," Jim murmured.

They returned to the apartment, where Emily was sitting silently with Mary.

Father Michael stepped forward, holding out the envelope.

"This is for you."

Emily snatched it from his hands and ran to her room.

The door clicked shut.

A moment of silence.

Then, the sound of paper tearing.

Jim and Mary sat there, holding their breath.

Inside the room, Emily's eyes blurred as she read the first line.

"My Dearest Emily..."

Chapter 21
A Heart-Wrenching Revelation

Emily sat on the edge of the bed, the dim light of the lamp casting a soft glow over the letter in her trembling hands. The room was quiet—too quiet, save for the sound of her uneven breathing.

Her name was written on the envelope in Father Joseph's familiar, steady handwriting.

She traced the ink with her fingertips, unwilling—afraid—to break the seal.

She took a deep breath, then, with hands that felt too weak to hold the weight of his final words, she tore open the envelope.

Her eyes skimmed the first few words.

My Dearest Emily,

By the time you read this, I will have gone home to the Father.

I wish I could be there to see you standing tall in your graduation robe, to watch you cross that stage with pride, and to bless you as you step into the life you have built with such resilience, strength, and grace.

I wish I could see the woman you have become—because, my child, you are remarkable.

I need to tell you something—something I should have told you long ago.

I have carried a burden for twenty years, and today, with these trembling hands, I will finally lay it down.

Emily, your mother never abandoned you.

Catherine Carter was a young woman who had the world stacked against her. She was lost, alone, and terrified when she walked into a motel room all those years ago. She had no one—no family, no home, no one to hold her hand.

I was there.

I heard her confession. I witnessed her pain. I promised her hope.

But, Emily... I failed her.

After she brought you into this world, when her family forced her to sign the adoption papers, I should have fought harder. I should have done more. But I was bound by my vows, by my limita-

tions as a priest, by the rules I was sworn to follow.

And because of that, you lost her. And she lost you.

I have spent two decades searching for a way to make that right.

And now, when I have so little time left, I have finally found her.

She never stopped thinking about you. She never stopped grieving the child that was taken from her. She never stopped wishing she had been strong enough to hold onto you.

I want you to meet your mother, Emily.

Not for me, but for you.

Because no matter how much I have loved you, no matter how much I have cherished being your "parent," there is a part of your heart that has longed for her.

And she has longed for you. Give her a chance, Emily.

If not today, then someday.

And when you see her—when you look into her eyes—know that it was never abandonment. It was never indifference.

It was pain. It was regret.

She was a mother who never stopped loving her child.

And if you ever wonder how much I have loved you—if you ever feel alone in this world—

remember this:

You were the greatest gift God ever placed in my life.

You were the daughter I never knew I needed.

And if I leave this world with nothing else, I leave with the joy of knowing you will be okay.

Live fully. Love deeply. Forgive where you can.

And when you do, think of me.

With all the love in my heart,

Your Parent,

Father Joseph

Her chest tightened with something she couldn't name—was it grief? Was it relief?

Was it the realization that her life had been built on a truth she had never known?

Her mother was alive. And Father Joseph had spent the last days of his life making sure she knew.

The tears came harder now, sobs shaking her small frame as she read a sentence again.

"You were the greatest gift God ever placed in my life."

Emily clutched the letter against her chest, pressing it to her heart like it could somehow bring him back.

Processing the Truth

She didn't know how long she sat there, letting the letter crush her soul and put it back together all at once.

The pain was all-consuming.

It wasn't anger toward Father Joseph—how could she ever feel anger toward the man who had saved her?

But there was something else—something that made her stomach twist, and her fingers dig into the sheets.

A rage she had buried for years—toward the people who forced this life upon her.

Toward the parents who tore Catherine apart, forcing her to give up her child.

Toward the system that let her slip away, moving her from home to home as though she were nothing more than a number.

Toward the universe itself, for making her an orphan when she had a mother out there—a mother who had wanted her.

And yet, beneath the rage, there was something even more terrifying.

Fear. A raw, bone-deep fear.

She had spent so many years believing she was unwanted.

Believing that her mother never looked for her.

Now, Father Joseph's letter had unraveled that story, leaving her with one aching question.

What if she met Catherine... and what if it was too late to fix what had been broken?

The Final Secret

A soft knock on the door.

Emily didn't respond.

Mary pushed the door open just a little, her voice gentle.

"Emily?"

She couldn't speak.

Her throat felt tight, her body felt drained and hollow.

Mary and Jim stepped inside, their expressions full of sorrow. They could see the way her face was swollen from crying, the way she clutched Joseph's letter like a lifeline.

Mary sat beside her on the bed, placing a warm hand over Emily's cold fingers.

"Sweetheart, we need to tell you something."

Emily's gaze didn't shift. She was too lost, too numb.

Jim exhaled, running a hand through his hair.

"Emily... we know where your mother is."

Her entire body went still.

The silence was so thick that for a moment, they could hear only the distant sound of the rain outside.

Finally, Emily blinked, her lips parting. "What?"

Jim and Mary exchanged a glance.

Jim spoke first. "Your mother, Catherine... she's alive. We've found her."

Emily's heart lurched. Her entire world shifted again—but this time, she had no idea where it would land.

Shock. Disbelief. A flicker of something she didn't dare name.

Hope? No. It was too dangerous to hope.

Her voice barely came out. "You... you found her?"

Mary squeezed her hand. "Yes, sweetheart. And she wants to see you."

Emily felt her chest tighten. She wanted to see her?

The mother who had lost her? The mother she had spent a lifetime pretending didn't exist? Because it was easier to believe she had never wanted her in the first place.

She swallowed. Her voice came out hoarse. "I don't know if I can do this."

Jim's voice was soft but firm. "You don't have to decide now. But, Emily... she's waiting for you."

A Candle for Father Joe

She's waiting for you. The words echoed in her mind, sinking deeper and deeper into her soul.

She closed her eyes, pressing the heels of her hands against her temples.

Father Joseph had spent his last moments bringing her back to the mother she lost.

Could she ignore that? Could she walk away now when he had given everything to bring her to this moment?

Could she live the rest of her life knowing she turned her back on the one thing Father Joseph had wanted for her?

She let out a shaky breath. "I need time," she whispered.

Mary nodded. "Take all the time you need."

Jim's voice was steady, patient. "But when you're ready... we'll take you to her."

Emily stood motionless, her breath caught between fear and something that felt like hope.

Then, slowly, as if guided by something beyond herself, she turned and walked into the small private chapel Father Joseph had kept like a sanctuary. The room was dim and quiet—just a flickering candle and the familiar scent of melted wax and incense lingering in the air.

She knelt on the cushioned bench.

Her heart still ached. Her hands trembled.

In that sacred stillness, something in her finally began to uncoil.

The walls no longer felt like walls. They felt like arms. It was as if Father Joseph's presence surrounded her—calm, warm, reassuring. She felt wrapped in something gentle... something holy.

A whisper seemed to rise inside her—not from outside, not from the walls or the room, but from her soul.

"It's time."

Her gaze dropped to the letter still crumpled in her hand, its edges worn now by tears and trembling fingers.

She pressed it to her chest, and for the first time since she had read it, Emily let herself exhale.

Not just air. But fear. Anger. Doubt.

And then she whispered the words that had been buried for so long.

"I want to meet my mother."

Chapter 22
Catherine's Breaking Point

The small apartment was dimly lit, and the quiet hum of the ceiling fan was the only sound in the otherwise empty, suffocating silence.

Catherine sat by the window, a cold cup of coffee untouched on the table beside her.

The city stretched before her, lights flickering in distant windows, but she saw none of it.

Her mind was trapped in the past—a past she had spent years trying to outrun, bury, forget.

And yet, here it was.

Unshakable. Unforgiving.

Her daughter was alive.

And she had the chance—the first real chance in twenty years—to reach out.

So why hadn't she? Why had she let the days slip by since Jim and Mary told her that Emily was waiting?

Why did she still feel paralyzed by the same fear that had once stolen her child from her arms?

. . .

The Weight of Lost Time

She let out a slow breath, her fingers tightening into fists.

She had spent so many years hating Father Joseph. Blaming him.

When she was young, that hate had kept her sane. It had been easier to turn her pain into rage—to convince herself that if he had just done more, just fought harder, she wouldn't have lost Emily.

But deep down, she knew the truth. He had tried.

In the days after her daughter was taken from her when she had been drowning in grief, he had reached out, offering help, comfort, and guidance.

And she had pushed him away because it was easier.

It was easier to blame him than to admit she had been too afraid to fight back against her family. Too scared to stand her ground.

She had been barely more than a child herself—a frightened girl abandoned by those who were supposed to love her.

She had fought back in every way she knew—rebellion, anger, recklessness.

But when it mattered most, she had been powerless. And the weight of that truth crushed her.

A sharp breath escaped her lips.

She had spent twenty years pretending she had made peace with it.

But now, sitting here, knowing Emily was alive, waiting, willing to meet her—

She realized she had made peace with nothing.

It had only been a mind game—a story she told herself to justify moving forward, to survive.

In a way, she was grateful for that illusion.

Because if she had truly faced the depth of her grief back then...

She might not have survived it.

The Breakdown

Her hands trembled as she stood up, moving to the small cabinet in the corner of the room.

She hesitated, then pulled out a worn shoebox, its lid barely holding together.

Inside—her only link to the past. A small pink hospital bracelet with "Baby Girl Carter" printed on it.

A single photograph—Emily as a newborn, taken by a nurse just before handing her over.

A crumpled note—Father Joseph's last attempt to reach her before she disappeared all those years ago.

Her breath hitched.

It was all she had left of her child.

She clenched her jaw, her vision blurring.

Twenty years of pain, of regret, of silent suffering—It all came crashing down.

The sob tore through her like a dam breaking.

She fell to her knees, clutching the tiny bracelet against her chest as if it could somehow bring back the past—as if it could undo everything.

Tears streamed down her face, heavy, uncontrollable, violent.

She had lost her daughter.

And now, for the first time, she allowed herself to mourn it. Allowed herself to feel the unbearable grief she had buried beneath layers of resentment and self-hatred.

"I'm sorry." The words spilled out, her voice breaking. "I'm so sorry, my baby."

She rocked back and forth, weeping, gasping, shaking. "I loved you. I loved you so much."

And for the first time, she admitted it.

It wasn't just Father Joseph. It wasn't just her parents.

She had let Emily go.

And that realization—that unbearable, inescapable truth—was the thing that shattered her completely.

A Decision That Cannot Wait

The storm of tears slowly subsided, leaving Catherine hollow and exhausted.

She stayed there, on the floor, for what felt like hours.

And then—clarity.

She couldn't run anymore. She couldn't undo the past.

But she could fight for what was left of the future.

She stood up, wiping her face. She reached for her phone, her fingers trembling as she dialed the only number that mattered now.

It rang.

Once.

Twice.

"Hello?"

Jim's voice on the other end was cautious, uncertain.

Catherine swallowed hard.

"Jim," she whispered. "I'm ready to meet my daughter."

Chapter 23
A Collision of Pain and Love

The small café was nearly empty, the late afternoon light casting long shadows across the polished wooden floors. A soft hum of conversation filled the space and the occasional clinking of cups punctuating the silence.

But at one table near the window, silence wasn't just present—it was suffocating.

Emily sat stiffly, her hands clenched around her coffee cup, though she hadn't taken a sip. Across from her, Catherine sat frozen, gripping the table's edge as if it was the only thing keeping her steady.

It had been seconds since they sat down.

But it felt like a lifetime.

A Wound Torn Open

Emily's heart pounded in her ears, drowning out the sound of the world around her. She had imagined this moment a thousand times—but never like this.

She didn't know what to say.

And apparently, neither did Catherine.

The tension stretched, a fragile thread pulling tight between them, ready to snap at any second.

Then, finally—Catherine broke the silence.

"I never wanted to lose you."

Her voice was soft—too soft. As if the words themselves were made of glass, they would shatter as soon as they left her lips.

Emily's jaw tightened.

A sharp, bitter laugh escaped her, but there was no humor in it. Only pain.

"But you did."

Catherine flinched as if she had been slapped.

Emily leaned forward, her eyes burning. The storm inside her had been brewing for twenty years, and now—it exploded.

"You know, lady, my childhood was a torture chamber."

Her voice trembled with raw fury.

"Mental. Physical. Emotional. A living hell."

Catherine sucked in a sharp breath, but Emily was already lost to the tidal wave of emotions.

"Every night, I cried myself to sleep, wondering why no one wanted me. Why didn't I have a mother to tuck me in, to hold me when I was scared? Do you know what it's like to be a child, alone in a cold bed, feeling like you don't belong anywhere?"

Catherine's eyes glossed over, her lips parting, but she couldn't speak.

Emily's voice rose, shaking with every word.

"Nobody cared if I was hungry. Nobody asked if I wanted anything special. I watched other kids at school—laughing, going home to parents who loved them. I wore hand-me-downs from strangers, carried a secondhand bag with someone else's name scribbled on the inside. Because that's what I was—a leftover. A forgotten child in the system."

Catherine's face crumpled, silent tears slipping down her cheeks.

But Emily wasn't done.

"Nobody told me what it meant to grow up, what to watch out for. Nobody taught me about love, about relationships, about how they could destroy you if you weren't careful. Nobody warned me about drugs, about alcohol, about the dark places you go to when life doesn't care about you. And so I tried it all. Every bad thing you can think of, I did."

Her voice cracked.

"Because I had nothing to lose."

The café around them seemed to disappear.

Catherine had brought a shaking hand to her mouth, unable to hold back the sob that had been rising in her throat.

Emily exhaled a ragged breath, her body trembling with exhaustion.

And then she whispered the words that cut the deepest.

"If it weren't for Father Joseph, I would have been dead by now, a rotting body on the street corner."

Catherine let out a quiet, choked cry.

Her head bowed, her shoulders shaking.

Emily saw it—the devastation, the regret, the years of guilt Catherine had been carrying.

But it didn't undo the years of her suffering. It didn't erase her scars.

And so, without another word—she stood up.

Catherine looked up quickly.

"Emily—"

But she was already walking away, pushing through the

door, stepping into the cool evening air, leaving Catherine behind in the ruins of her grief.

Moment of Truth

She didn't move.

Not when Emily walked out.

Not when the door swung shut behind her.

Not when the weight of twenty years crushed her like an avalanche.

Her hands shook as she reached for the napkin in front of her, gripping it tightly in her fist, as if somehow—somehow—it could hold her together.

Emily's words echoed in her mind, each as a dagger to her soul.

She had suffered. She had been left behind, abandoned, forgotten.

And Catherine... Catherine had let it happen.

She pressed a shaking hand to her chest, a quiet sob slipping past her lips.

There was no Father Joseph to rescue her now.

She had lost her daughter.

But this time—she wasn't going to let go.

She needed Emily as much as Emily needed her.

And she would fight for her.

A Moment of Reflection

That night, Emily sat alone in her apartment.

The silence felt different.

Not empty. Not numb. Just... heavy.

She reached for the envelope beside her bed—Father Joseph's letter.

She had already read it several times. But tonight—she needed it again.

Her hands trembled as she unfolded the paper, his words wrapping around her like an embrace from beyond.

"If you ever wonder how much I have loved you, remember this: You were the greatest gift God ever placed in my life."

A choked sound escaped her throat.

Her vision blurred, tears falling silently onto the page.

Joseph had spent his last moments fighting for her.

Fighting for her to have this chance. Fighting for her to have a mother.

She closed her eyes, her heart aching.

I can't let this chance slip away.

She pressed the letter to her chest, breathing deeply.

Tomorrow—she would go back.

Not because she had to. But because she wanted to.

Healing Begins

Catherine sat at the same café, her hands wrapped around a cup of tea that had long gone cold.

She wasn't sure if Emily would come. She barely dared to hope.

The pain of yesterday's encounter still clung to her like a heavy fog—Emily's anger, her accusations, her raw suffering laid bare.

And the worst part? Catherine knew she was right.

She had deserved every word. She had failed her daughter.

And yet—she was here.

Because no matter how much time had passed, no

matter how deep the scars ran—Catherine wasn't going to lose her again.

Then—the bell over the café door jingled.

Her breath caught in her throat. She looked up.

And Emily was there. This time, she came back.

For a moment, neither moved.

Then, slowly, Emily stepped forward.

Catherine's hands trembled as she set down her cup, swallowing hard.

She didn't dare speak first. So Emily did.

"I don't know if I can forgive everything today."

Catherine's heart stopped.

But then—Emily exhaled. "But I want to try. And I will try. And I am sorry for the outburst yesterday."

A choked sob escaped Catherine's lips.

Emily sat down across from her, and this time—there was no anger in her eyes.

Just hesitation. Caution. A fragile willingness to listen.

Catherine took a shaky breath. This was her chance.

She reached across the table, but stopped herself, resting her hands just an inch from Emily's.

And then—she began to speak.

Chapter 24
The Truth After Twenty Years

The Truth After Twenty Years

"Emily," she started, her voice barely above a whisper. "I never wanted to let you go."

Emily's fingers tightened around her coffee cup. She said nothing.

So Catherine continued, her words heavy, halting.

"I fought, I really did. But I was barely eighteen, alone, terrified, and drowning in shame. Abandoned by an insensitive, selfish man. My parents... they weren't kind, Emily. They told me I had ruined everything. That keeping you would destroy my life. That I was selfish for even thinking about it."

Her eyes shimmered with unshed tears.

Her throat tightened.

"They tore you away from my hands days after you were born. They didn't let me hold you ever since, not even once. I begged them, Emily, I begged them."

Emily's lips parted slightly.

Catherine clenched her hands into fists.

"And then, you were gone."

A single tear slipped down her cheek.

"I tried to run away, to find you. But they told me it was too late. That you had already been adopted, placed in a good home, that I had to move on."

She laughed bitterly, shaking her head.

"But I couldn't. I couldn't just forget you. I couldn't pretend like you didn't exist. I felt like a ghost, walking through life, just waiting—waiting for some way to find you again."

Emily's breathing hitched.

"But, what can a helpless eighteen-year-old do?" Catherine looked away, her voice a frayed whisper.

"After that, everything felt... hollow. I had no home. I lived in shelters, slept on couches, took odd jobs to stay afloat. For years, I cleaned motel bathrooms, waited tables, anything that paid enough to eat and not freeze. But I never stopped thinking about you."

She looked up, meeting Emily's eyes for the first time since she began.

"Every birthday, I wondered where you were. Every Christmas, I cried over a name I couldn't say aloud. And every single night, I prayed God would give me one more chance. Just one. Not to explain. Not even to be forgiven. Just... to see you again."

Emily's chest tightened, her breath unsteady.

Catherine smiled sadly, her voice quiet.

"The only thing that kept me going was the hope that someday... I'd find you. That's what got me through every miserable shift, every dark alley, every time I had no place to sleep..... Hope."

A tear slid down her cheek.

"And now you're here, sitting in front of me... and I'm terrified all over again."

Emily's lip trembled. She swallowed hard and looked away.

For the first time, her anger gave way to something else.

Grief. Recognition. And the beginning of something neither of them had dared to name—mercy.

"And I remember, Father Joseph had sent me a note."

Emily's eyes snapped up.

"He wanted me to fight for you. But, Emily, I was already broken. I was too weak, and had no connections. I couldn't see a way back. I... I ran away."

Her tears fell freely now.

Emily sat frozen, her chest rising and falling quickly.

Catherine shook her head.

"I know you'll never understand what that was like. And you don't have to."

Catherine slowly took Emily's hand, "You suffered because I wasn't strong enough. I failed you. And for that, I will never, ever stop being sorry."

She took a shaky breath.

"But if you let me, I want to make it right."

A Moment of Grace

Emily looked away, blinking hard against the tears forming in her eyes.

Her heart felt like it was splitting open.

Her entire life, she had believed one story: That her mother didn't want her.

That she had been discarded.

That she had never been loved.

But now—Catherine's story changed everything.

Catherine had loved her.

She had just been too broken to fight.

Emily closed her eyes.

Joseph's words flashed through her mind—words written just for her.

"If you ever wonder how much I have loved you, remember this: You were the greatest gift God ever placed in my life."

Her throat tightened.

This was what he had wanted for her.

Not just to know the truth—but to find her mother again.

And so, at that moment, Emily made her choice.

She looked up, her eyes red, and whispered, "I don't know how to do this."

Catherine let out a shaky laugh, wiping her tears. "Me neither."

A silence stretched between them.

And then, hesitantly, Emily reached across the table, placing her hand over Catherine's.

Catherine let out a quiet sob.

And just like that—something shifted.

The years of separation, the heartbreak, the suffering—it didn't disappear.

But for the first time in twenty years, it wasn't insurmountable.

Catherine squeezed her hand.

"Can I hug you?" she asked, her voice barely above a whisper.

Emily hesitated—just for a second.

Then, slowly—she nodded.

Catherine stood up, tears streaming down her face.

And as she pulled Emily into her arms—her daughter, her baby girl—Emily didn't pull away.

She let herself be held.

And for the first time she felt what it was like to be in the arms of a mother who loved her.

Chapter 25
A Tribute to Father Joseph

The sun hung low in the sky, casting a golden glow over St. John's parish church. The stone walls, weathered by time, stood as silent witnesses to the man who had walked these grounds for decades—offering hope, guidance, and love.

Today, those doors stood open wide as if stretching out their arms to welcome the flock once more—this time, for a final farewell—a Memorial Mass for Father Joseph, a special tribute to him, with the Bishop officiating.

They would be there.

The people who had once filled the pews to attend his Mass and hear his homilies.

The children he had baptized.

The couples whose vows he had blessed.

The lost souls he had comforted.

The outcasts he had embraced.

All of them, drawn not by duty, but by love—

To remember. To honor.

To say, quietly and with tears, "Thank you."

A Candle for Father Joe

* * *

That morning, before the Memorial Mass, Emily opened the door of Father Joseph's apartment for Catherine—their first meeting after their reconciliation.

It was a strange feeling—welcoming her mother into a space that once belonged to the man who had been her only "parent."

The room still smelled faintly of fresh flowers as it always did, of candle wax, and the faintest trace of his aftershave lingering in the air.

Catherine stood by the bookshelf, her fingers lightly touching the worn leather bindings of the volumes Father Joseph had loved.

"This was his world," Emily murmured.

Catherine nodded. "And for a time, he was ours too."

Emily looked at her mother, studying her face—the quiet pain, the hope, the regret, the longing.

It was still new. Still delicate.

But she was willing to try.

"Come sit," she said, motioning to the couch. "Tell me something about yourself."

Catherine's eyebrows lifted in mild surprise. "What do you want to know?"

Emily shrugged. "Anything. I don't really know you."

And so, for the first time, they sat together—not as two strangers bound by the past, but as a mother and daughter cautiously stepping into something new.

They talked.

Not about apologies or the past they couldn't change—but about childhood memories, favorite books, and the music Catherine used to dance to when no one was watching.

Emily heard her mother's voice free from grief for the first time—light, even wistful. A young girl's voice still tucked beneath the weary tones of a woman who had survived too much, too soon.

As Catherine spoke, her story gently unfolded—a life raised in noise but not in love. Parents who partied more than they parented. A house always full of people but empty of warmth.

"They were good at appearances," she said quietly. "But not much else."

With time, she drifted—first to the closet, talking to her toys, then into her friends' homes and into their choices.

She didn't call it rebellion—just gravitation.

No one was holding her down, so she fell. Into late-night escapades, bad decisions, desperate attention-seeking, and eventually, the arms of someone who said he loved her —until he didn't.

It wasn't a confession.

It was simply the truth—laid bare in the soft light of the apartment that had once belonged to the man who brought them back together.

Emily listened silently, piecing together fragments of a girl she'd never known. It wasn't easy. It didn't erase the pain. But it opened a small window into understanding.

And somehow, in that quiet moment, the air between them began to soften—not into something whole, not yet. But into something new.

Later, as Emily walked out the door with her mother beside her, heading to the church for Father Joseph's Memorial Mass, she felt it.

A shift.
Small. Subtle. But real.

It was as though something heavy she'd carried for years had lightened—just enough to take a deeper breath.

* * *

A Church Full of Love

The church was full. More than Emily had expected.

She and Catherine sat near the front, beside Jim and Mary. As Emily looked around, she saw so many familiar faces.

The parishioners who had once greeted Father Joseph every Sunday.

The volunteers from the Outreach Center.

People from every stage of his life.

All of them were there, because he had changed them.

The organ's deep chords filled the space. The Bishop, with Father Michael alongside him, stepped up to the altar and celebrated Mass, the same Mass Father Joseph had celebrated on the same altar numerous times for others.

After reading the Gospel, the Bishop's eyes scanned the congregation before he spoke.

"We are here to honor a man whose love knew no boundaries. Father Joseph Thomas was more than a priest—he was a shepherd, a healer, a refuge for the lost. His heart was never closed to those who suffered. And today, a week after his departure, we do not mourn his death. We celebrate his life, believing what we heard in our First Reading, "The souls of the just are in the hands of God."

Emily bowed her head, her throat tightening. He was right. This wasn't about grief. This was about gratitude.

He had lived well. And because of that, so many of them had lived better.

. . .

Jim's Remembrance

After Mass, the congregation moved to the Parish Hall for a small reception.

People shared stories. Laughed. Even cried.

Then Jim stepped up to the podium. He cleared his throat, his voice thick with emotion.

"I had the privilege of knowing Father Joseph not just as a priest, but as a friend. And if you knew him, you knew he was the kind of man who carried people's burdens as if they were his own. No matter what you were going through, he was there. And somehow, no matter how much pain you were in, you always left him feeling a little lighter."

A murmur of agreement swept through the hall.

Jim looked over at Emily. "And some people here, more than others, know exactly what I mean."

Emily stood up. Her heart pounded.

She hadn't planned to speak. But how could she not?

She walked to the podium, facing the people who had loved him.

She took a deep breath. "Father Joseph was the reason I am standing here today."

A hush fell over the room.

"I was lost. He found me. I was broken. He helped me heal. And when I thought I had no one, he became my family. He was my "parent." **Someone like him— every child should have."**

Her voice wavered, but she kept going.

"I don't think he ever truly knew the depth of what he did for people. He just... did it. Because that's who he was. But today, if he's listening, I want him to know... his love didn't die with him. It lives on. In me. In all of us. And I will carry it forward."

Her vision blurred as she stepped down.

Jim patted her shoulder gently, his own eyes wet.

And Emily knew—this was what Father Joseph would have wanted.

One Last Candle

As the day came to a close, Emily and Catherine walked together to Father Joseph's tomb.

A simple stone. A simple inscription.

"Servant of Christ. Shepherd of the Lost. A Father to many."

Emily knelt, pulling out a small candle, striking a match just as she had done a week ago. The flame flickered against the evening light.

Catherine knelt beside her, lighting her own candle.

They watched in silence, the glow dancing between them.

The wind stirred the leaves around them, whispering through the trees.

And now, Emily didn't feel that deep ache of loss.

She felt peace.

Epilogue
A Candle, And Another......

The air was crisp with the scent of autumn, the leaves swirling in golden and amber hues around the stone path leading to the Marian grotto, outside the church. A soft breeze rustled through the trees, whispering secrets known only to time.

Emily walked beside her mother, their steps slow, reverent. It had been exactly one year since Father Joseph left them—left this world, but never their hearts.

The grotto stood just as she remembered it—the place where Catherine had once knelt, seeking hope in the depths of her own despair.

The place where Father Joseph had first met her mother.

The place where everything had begun.

A few candles flickered at the base of the statue of the Virgin Mary, placed by someone who, like them, had come seeking solace.

Emily took a deep breath, her fingers curling around the small white candle she held.

Catherine stood beside her, silent, reflective.

A Candle for Father Joe

They had spoken so much over the past year—of the past, of regrets, of love, of healing.

But now, in this moment, no words were needed.

Emily knelt, carefully placing the candle among the others.

She struck a match, the flame sparking to life, dancing in the gentle evening wind, her heart filled with a profound sense of gratitude.

She closed her eyes and whispered, "Thank you, Father. You didn't just save me. You gave me a life."

A single tear slid down her cheek, but this time, it wasn't from pain.

It was from love. From peace. From the understanding that Father Joseph's kindness had been the thread that wove her life back together.

She had spent years searching for love, for purpose, for belonging.

And he had been there all along—guiding her, believing in her, loving her.

Emily exhaled slowly and opened her eyes.

And that's when she saw her.

A girl—no older than she had been at sixteen—kneeling a few feet away.

She had dark eyes, wide with uncertainty, her hands clasped tightly in prayer.

Emily recognized the look. The way she had once been.

She felt a pull—a deep, knowing pull.

She turned toward Catherine, who had also noticed the girl. Her mother met her gaze, understanding instantly.

This was what Father Joseph had lived for.

For those who felt unseen. For those who had nowhere to go.

For those who needed someone to reach out first.

Emily hesitated only a moment.

Then, with a soft smile, she stepped forward.

She knelt beside the girl, gently touching her shoulder.

The girl looked up, startled.

Emily's voice was gentle, steady, and filled with warmth.

"Are you okay?"

And in that moment, as the candle flickered beside them, **Father Joseph's legacy lived on.**

The Bright Light

He was just one man.

But his love—his compassion—was enough to change a life.

And that life would go on to change another.

And another.

And another.

Until the world itself was a little brighter, a little kinder, a little more filled with love.

THE END

Afterword

A Candle for Father Joe began as a quiet ache in my heart—a story that didn't arrive fully formed, but unfolded slowly, like the flicker of a light in the dark. It was born from years of pastoral ministry, walking beside people whose lives were marked by brokenness, healing, second chances, and the power of grace.

In Joseph, I see many priests I have known: kind, flawed, burdened by silent regrets, yet quietly faithful. In Emily, I see countless young people searching for belonging, hope, and someone who believes in them. And in Catherine, I see the ache of mothers who loved deeply but were never given the space to show it.

This novel is fiction—but the emotions it carries are very real. It is my tribute to those who have loved imperfectly, who have wrestled with regret, and who, despite it all, still choose to light one small candle and keep walking forward.

If this story has touched you, I am grateful. If it has stirred a memory, a tear, or a glimmer of hope, then perhaps —like Father Joseph—you too have carried light for someone who needed it.

Afterword

Thank you for reading.
— **Rev. Jose Kallukalam**

About the Author

Rev. Jose Kallukalam is a retired Catholic pastor and seasoned writer whose ministry has spanned over five decades across continents. Drawing deeply from his pastoral experiences walking alongside families through joy, heartbreak, and healing, his novels blend emotional honesty with spiritual depth.

After being ordained priest in Kerala, India, he pursued graduate studies in 'Religious Communication' at Loyola University Chicago before returning to his home diocese,

About the Author

where he served as Director of Communication Media. In this role, he produced television programs and stage productions and penned hundreds of song lyrics, many of which can be found on his YouTube channel, Harmony of Life.

A Candle for Father Joe is his most personal and poignant work yet—a reflection on second chances, the power of compassion, and the quiet redemption that shapes the human spirit.

Also by Jose Kallukalam

Strategic Pastoral Planning

Mission Driven Pastoral Ministry

Upcoming Book

'Living Well, Aging Well'- A Parctical Guide to Aging with Wisdom and Vitality.

Upcoming Novel

'The Flame and The Lion' - The Empire Roared, and The Church Whispered Back. A Christian Historical Novel set in the shadow of Nero's madness and the rise of the early Christian movement. The story of a former Zealot and one of the disciples who met the Risen Christ on the road to Emmaus—and his sister Esther, whose quiet faith becomes a force that outlives empires.

N.B. If you liked this book, please write s review on amamzon.com